LOVE OF THE GAME

JOHN COY

FEIWEL AND FRIENDS
NEW YORK

A FEIWEL AND FRIENDS BOOK
An Imprint of Macmillan

Library of Congress Cataloging-in-Publication Data

Coy, John,
Love of the game / John Coy. — 1st ed.
p. cm.
Summary: Sixth-grader Jackson has a rough start in middle school,
with bullies on the bus, few classes with his friends, and changes at home,
but some good teachers, meeting a girl, joining a club,
and playing football soon turn things around.
[1. Middle schools—Fiction.   2. Schools—Fiction.   3. Interpersonal
relations—Fiction.   4. Family life—Fiction.]   I. Title.
PZ7.C839455Lov 2011
[Fic]—dc22
2010050897

ISBN: 978-0-312-37331-3 (hardcover)
10 9 8 7 6 5 4 3 2 1

ISBN: 978-1-250-00637-0 (paperback)
10 9 8 7 6 5 4 3 2 1

Book design by Tim Hall

Feiwel and Friends logo designed by Filomena Tuosto

First Edition: 2011

10 9 8 7 6 5 4 3 2 1

mackids.com

For Patrick

CHAPTER 1

Where on earth is the bus?

I step out into the street and squint into the sun. I check my phone. 7:33. It's supposed to be here.

Behind me two older girls with straight, black hair, one with purple nail polish and the other with blue, ignore me completely as they argue about whether somebody named Rex is hot.

Where's the bus? You'd think they'd make sure it was on time on the first day of middle school. I've already got enough to worry about with lockers, schedules, and the awful things eighth graders are dreaming up to do to us.

I check my phone again. 7:33. How can that be? It feels like ten minutes have passed. I smooth down my new gold Nike T-shirt. Dad tried to get me to wear the new jeans we bought last week, but I told him you don't want to overdo it on the first day of middle school. You can't look like you're trying too hard.

7:34. The bus is late. The first day is pressure enough without showing up after the bell. The bus driver should be fired. I hear a low rumbling. Coming around the corner is the orange box on wheels that means summer is officially over.

I shove my phone in my backpack and listen to the two girls. They've finally found a subject they can agree on: Logan. "Stay away from him. He'll pretend to be nice but will stab you in the back."

As the bus pulls up, I wish my best friend Gig was on it. We rode the same bus for six years to elementary school, but now we're on different routes. I never thought I'd admit it, but I could use some of his stupid jokes right now.

The bus door opens and I freeze. All of a sudden I don't want to get on. My feet feel superglued to the sidewalk.

"Move it." One of the girls pushes me in the back.

As I climb the steps I'm shocked to see that the bus is already jam packed. Kids are squished together three to a seat, talking and laughing.

"Find a seat." The bus driver, who's got bushy hair popping out of a baseball hat, points over his shoulder. He's playing country music that sounds like it's about a hundred years old.

I move farther back and feel the eyes of every seventh and eighth grader sizing me up. The competing perfumes, colognes, and deodorant mingle together. Other kids must have been like me and kept putting it on.

Halfway back my friend Isaac is mashed up against a window. "I didn't know you were on this bus."

"Jackson?" He's squeezed in by two boys who take up the rest of the seat.

"Save me a place tomorrow."

"Sixers can't save seats." The boy on the aisle has peanut butter breath. He pushes me and I fall against a girl with glasses and try to regain my balance.

Two girls with eye shadow so heavy they look like raccoons check their phones. I don't want to sit with girls, but I don't want to keep going back either.

"Can I sit here?" I try to sound friendly.

"No!" The girls don't even look up.

"That's my seat." The girl with purple nail polish pushes past me.

"We need everybody sitting down," the bus driver hollers.

With every step back I feel like I'm being sucked into the

eighth-grade black hole. The boys back here are bigger and tougher and some of them are swearing every other word.

"Here's a seat," a boy wearing wraparound sunglasses calls from the rear. A blond kid with spiked hair sitting next to him laughs.

In the last seat of the bus on the left side, a gigantic guy is sitting all by himself. He's so big he must play football. He's so big he could be the entire left side of an offensive line.

"Can I sit down?"

He doesn't answer.

"Have a seat." The sunglasses kid shoves me against the huge guy who pushes me away. I get shoved back and forth between them like a Ping-Pong ball. Finally I turn my legs to the side and hold my hands out in front of me.

"Sixer?" Sunglasses asks.

"What?" I look to the bus driver, but he's not paying any attention.

"Are you in sixth grade?"

"Yeah."

"The back is reserved for eighth graders." His voice is raspy and he looks a lot older, like maybe he flunked a couple of grades. "What do you have for rent?"

"What?"

4

"Sixers pay rent back here. What do you have for money?"

"I don't have any money." I hold out my hands.

"That's baaaaaaad." The way he stretches it out sounds worse.

"What do you have for food?" The spike-haired kid leans over.

"Just my lunch."

"Hand it over," Sunglasses says.

I take off my backpack and unzip it as the bus driver turns a corner and the big guy falls into me and almost knocks me off the seat. We're not picking anybody else up, so my stop must be the last one.

"Hurry up," Spike Head commands. "I'm starving."

I take out my lunch and Sunglasses swipes it out of my hands. He pulls out potato chips, Oreo cookies, and cheese and crackers.

"What's this?" He makes a face as he pulls open my sandwich.

"Tur . . . tur . . . turkey and sun-dried tomato."

"Nasty." He throws it on the floor and stomps on it with his boot. "Bring better food tomorrow . . . or else." He holds up the plastic bag of carrot and celery sticks. "Do I look like a rabbit?"

"No."

He tosses the bag at me as he and Spike Head shove cheese and crackers into their mouths. My stomach rumbles as the crackers crunch.

"We want brownies, Rice Krispie bars, and Twinkies tomorrow," Spike Head says with food falling out of his mouth.

"And rent money," Sunglasses adds. "Don't forget the money."

When the bus pulls up in front of the school, Isaac is waiting for me. "How bad was it back there?" He's wearing new black-and-red Nikes and an Under Armour shirt.

"Terrible." The entrance to Longview Middle School towers over us.

"Where you two losers been?" Gig rushes up and bumps into me.

"Our bus was late."

"Mine was right on time."

"Where's Diego?" Isaac asks.

"No clue," Gig says. "He doesn't ride the bus so I don't know how he's getting here."

Some of the students can't wait to get in, but others like us stand around outside soaking up the final seconds of freedom.

"I'm glad to have different teachers in middle school," Isaac says.

I remember Mrs. Spanier from last year. "We're not going to get stuck with one boring teacher."

"No, now we're going to have lots of boring teachers," Gig says. "I wish we could skip school and go straight to Echo Park for football."

"Me, too." I twirl the strap on my backpack. I'd love to smash into somebody on the football field right now.

"We're going to have a good team," Isaac says. "Diego's going to help us out."

"Wait and see," Gig says.

"What do you mean?" I ask.

"He hasn't done anything yet in football," Gig says. "He needs to prove himself."

When the bell rings, people push toward the entrance. I look around for Diego but can't find him. We're funneled to the door like cattle forced into a slaughterhouse.

A spitball whizzes past my head. A sweaty kid elbows me and shoves me aside. I'm not even in the building yet, and I've got a bad feeling about middle school.

Chapter 2

The shiny halls of Longview are swarming with students. There should be about twice as much space to fit everybody. Because it's jam-packed, people bump into each other accidentally, but some of the bigger kids bang around on purpose.

I stick close to Gig and Isaac as we find the locker area in the sixth-grade section. I turn my palm over to where I've written 1321 and 26-29-3. I repeat the numbers to myself trying to memorize them.

I get a moment of panic at 1321 as Gig and Isaac keep going to their lockers. I'm on my own in middle school. I drop my backpack down and spin the combination while checking the numbers on my hand.

My locker won't open.

I try it again, but it still won't open.

I rub my sweaty palms together and try it again. No luck.

If I can't get my locker open, I'm in big trouble. I stare at the numbers that have started to smear. Clockwise twice around to twenty-six, then the other way past twenty-six to twenty-nine, then directly back to three.

It won't open.

Next to me, a girl's checking her hair in the sparkly mirror of her decorated door. On the other side, a boy slams his locker shut. I'd like to ask them for help, but I'd feel like a complete loser.

I try again, but I still can't get mine open. I kick at my backpack. We can't bring backpacks to class, so right away I'll be in trouble. I'll get detention on the first day of school.

"Hey, Jackson." Diego comes up.

"My locker won't open."

"Let me try." He's wearing a new soccer jersey and a back-to-school haircut.

I show him my palm and he spins the dial quickly and it opens part way, but jams on the side. Diego grabs the top and gives a muscle-man pull.

"How did you get it open?"

"Yank on it."

"No, I mean the numbers."

"Easy. Just once past twenty-six," he says. "When you get to twenty-six, slow down so you can stop on twenty-nine right away."

"Thanks." I want to try it again right away, but I don't want to close it and not get it open. I pull out my planner, binder, pencils, notebooks, and folders and shove my backpack in.

"Nork and San," Gig says as he and Isaac come up carrying their binders.

"What?" My locker sticks on the edge so I bang on it.

"You need nicknames in middle school," Gig says. "Everybody knows that. I've got a good one, but we all need 'em. That's why starting now you'll be Nork and Diego will be San."

"Nork?"

"Yeah, remember? It's a combination of nerd and dork."

"I'm not going to be Nork."

"You're a perfect Nork," Gig says. "San is fine with his name. San Diego."

"No way," Diego says. "*San* means 'saint' in Spanish. I'm no saint."

"It's still a good nickname." Gig smirks.

"What are you?" I ask Isaac.

"Ike. My cousins call me that."

"I like Ike," Gig says. "What about you, Nork?"

"Don't call me Nork."

"Nork fits. You look like a nork."

"Knock it off, you two." Isaac holds up his hands. "Did you know homeroom is mixed grades?"

"Yeah," Diego says. "They're putting us in with seventh and eighth graders right away."

"That's stupid." I set my stuff on the floor since we're gathered in a group like a lot of other kids in the hall. "Don't they realize we only want to be with sixth graders?"

"Yeah," says Isaac. "I probably won't know anyone in there."

Isaac originally was going to go to Eagle Bluff rather than Longview. I don't want a bad first day changing his mind.

"What do you all have first period?" Isaac asks.

Diego checks his planner. "American Studies."

"Language arts." Gig frowns.

I pick up my planner. "Math. What do you have?"

"Language arts," Isaac says.

"With Gig?" I ask.

"No way." Gig smirks. "Ike's in Gifted and Talented."

"None of us are together," I say.

"Let's see your planner," Isaac says to me. "We're together for FACS."

"What's FACS?" Gig asks.

"Family and consumer science," Diego says. "You get to cook stuff and eat it. My brother says it's a good class, but I don't have it until next trimester. It rotates with art and industrial tech."

The warning bell rings and we all move toward our homerooms. I walk beside Gig. We've been best friends since kindergarten, but now we don't have a single class together.

"You boys better get a move on," one of the hall monitors warns. "If you're not in class by the bell, you'll get a tardy."

"Where's F-13?" Gig asks.

"Straight ahead." She points down the hall.

"What about E-28?" I ask.

"You're not even close. You've got to go back past the library and take a left. E-28 is down in the seventh-grade section."

I turn away from my friends. Why am I the only one with homeroom in a different part of the building?

I run toward the library but get caught by another hall monitor.

"No running or I'll write you up," she warns. "You need to give yourself plenty of time to get where you're going."

That's the problem. I don't know where I'm going, but I don't feel like asking her. I walk fast like one of those women who speed walk around the mall.

Finally I find the E section, but the numbers go from E-8 to E-15 without any pattern. This is the worst numbering system ever. The person who did this must have wanted to torture new students. I turn to the map in my planner, but the numbers are so small it's hard to read.

The halls have emptied now except for two guys coming toward me: Big and Huge. I try to act like I know where I'm going, but I feel like I've got a neon sign on my head that's flashing SIXER, SIXER, SIXER.

Big and Huge look at each other. They split up and Big walks to one side of me and Huge to the other.

"Sixer." Big turns and shoves me toward Huge.

I lose my balance and stagger against him.

"Get off me, Sixer." He pushes me.

Big shoves me back harder, and as I fall to the ground,

my planner, binder, and pencils go flying in different directions.

When the bell rings, they disappear. I gather up my stuff from the ground and follow the numbers.

E-19. E-21.

Middle school's officially begun: I'm late and I'm lost.

CHAPTER 3

"**Y**ou must be Jackson Kennedy," the teacher says when I finally find E-28, which is a science room.

"Yes." I search for a seat.

"I'm Ms. Constantine." She's got short dark hair and is wearing a necklace with chunky beads. "We make allowances the first day, but we expect you to be on time for homeroom." She says it in a firm way, and it's clear what she expects.

There's an open seat in back by a bunch of eighth-grade boys, but I'm not making that mistake again. Instead, I march right up front like I'm a little kindergartner.

"Hi, Jackson," Sydney, Gig's sister, says to me. She's a year younger than Gig, but because he got held back, they're in the same grade.

"Hey." It figures she'd be up front with the other brainiacs.

Secretly I'm glad she's here. It's nice to know at least one person.

Sydney's hair is pulled back in a turquoise headband and her skin is summertime tan, but something about her is different. She looks older, more like a middle school student. Around the room, all the students look more like they belong in middle school than I do.

"Remember, seventh and eighth graders"—Ms. Constantine holds up some forms—"if you are playing a fall sport, you need to have a physical and insurance information on file to be eligible."

Sydney raises her hand. "Why can't sixth graders play sports?"

"You can. You can play through the YMCA or through the Suburban Athletic League."

"But why can't we play for the school?" Sydney protests.

"We want sixth graders to focus on school," Ms. Constantine says. "I didn't make up the rules. Only seventh and eighth graders can play school sports."

"We're part of the school," Sydney says. "We shouldn't be treated like second-class citizens. We should be able to play for Longview, too."

Sydney's speaking up like she did in fifth grade. She's not

acting like she's intimidated by being in middle school or being around seventh and eighth graders. Maybe it's different if you're a girl. Maybe it's different if you're Sydney.

"What fall sport are you going to play?" she whispers to me as Ms. Constantine passes out forms.

"Football. I'm all signed up. What are you going to play?"

"I'm still deciding between volleyball and soccer." She smiles. "Maybe football."

"You're not." I can't believe it. Sydney came out for baseball last spring and Gig completely lost it. I'm not going through that again.

"Girls can play football," she says.

"I know. That doesn't mean you should."

"It means I have the choice."

"What are you two discussing?" Ms. Constantine comes over to our table.

"Nothing," I mumble.

"Discrimination against sixth graders," Sydney says.

"Take out your planners," she says. "We want to be sure you know where you're going."

I open mine up. Sydney's probably not serious about football, but I'm not sure. I never know what she's going to do.

I don't have any friends in my first two classes, math and language arts, but I'm relieved they are back in the sixth-grade section. Both teachers talk about their high expectations for the trimester, but in math, Mr. Tedesco actually gives us homework. Homework on the first day of school? That's messed up.

In language arts, Ms. Tremont, who stands super-straight like a stick figure, says that we're expected to read thirty minutes outside of class each day and write down in a reading log what we're reading. After we finish complaining, she says we can read anything we want, including magazines, graphic novels, even stuff online. She says it's reading for fun and that it's important we have choices.

"Does it count if we watch a movie that's based on a book?" Noah Hauser asks.

"No, I've got a broad definition of reading, but reading still means reading words."

"What about texting?" another kid asks.

"Do you read words when you text?"

"Yeah," we all say.

"Then that counts as reading. Write it in your log." Ms. Tremont moves around the room. "But I want you to experiment. Try some new things with your reading."

Reading thirty minutes a day outside of school sounded impossible, but if reading online and texting count, maybe I'm reading more than I think.

By the time I get to general music, I'm so glad to have a class with a friend that I rush over to grab the seat next to Diego before anybody else can. "What's up?"

"I already have homework."

"Me, too." I open up a new notebook. "Did you get your physical for football?"

Diego shakes his head.

"Why not?" I stare at him.

"I can't play on weekends. I work for my uncle then."

"I know you do. We don't play on weekends."

Diego clicks his mechanical pencil and looks away.

"Why didn't you get your physical?"

Diego sighs. "My mom doesn't want me to play. She's worried about how dangerous football is."

"Football's not that dangerous. You've got to persuade her. You promised us you'd play after we all agreed to go to soccer camp."

"I tried," Diego says.

"You've got to do more than try. We're counting on you."

"Settle down, class." A short guy with oversize glasses waves his hands at us. "I'm Mr. Corland and this is third period general music on Day One. We rotate with gym, so tomorrow on Day Two, you'll be there."

He takes attendance and hands out change slips for anybody who wants to switch to band or choir. From the way he talks it's clear that he thinks band and choir are superior to general music, but Diego and I both stay. I can't sing and there's no instrument I want to play.

Mr. Corland introduces our first unit, which is rhythm, and starts going on about whole notes, half notes, quarter notes, and eighth notes. He's one of those super-boring teachers. Maybe that's part of his master plan. Maybe he's trying to make general music unbearable so more people will switch to band or choir.

He drones on about the difference between notes and rests as I stare out the window.

"Let's try something different," he says. "Anybody who can come up to the board and spell *rhythm* correctly will get an A on this first unit."

Trenton Cromarty, who was with us in fifth grade, volunteers.

RITHM. That's not even close.

A girl I don't know raises her hand and goes to the board. RYTHEM.

As I look around the room, I realize most of the good students, like Isaac, are in band or choir. General music is for people who have no talent. But if I get this right, I've got an A for the unit and can kick back. I raise my hand and go to the board.

I write the R and pause. I know there's a Y in it.

RYTHM.

I stand back from the board and look to Mr. Corland, who's shaking his head.

A few more people try, but nobody gets it. Mr. Corland erases all the improper spellings and writes in big letters.

RHYTHM.

"Just as I suspected," he says. "You've all got a lot to learn." He underlines RHYTHM. "But we're going to have fun in here, too."

Teachers keep telling us we're going to have fun. They wouldn't have to say that if it was true.

CHAPTER 4

By the time the bell rings for lunch I'm starving. Diego and I hurry to our lockers, and I spin my combination the way he showed me. It opens, but jams again on the side.

"Stupid locker." I yank on it and it finally pops free. I shove my books, binder, and planner in and grab my lunch, which feels like nothing's in it.

"Hurry." Diego grabs my shirt.

When I shut the locker, it sticks again. I bang it closed. Everybody else got a decent locker and I've got one that's junk.

As we're walking as fast as we can, I see Isaac up ahead.

"Isaac!" I shout.

He turns and waits for us as all the sixth graders in the school pour into the cafeteria.

"Where's Gig?" he asks.

"I don't know."

"Over here," Diego shouts. "This is shorter."

I follow him and Isaac even though I've got my cold lunch. There's no way I'm sitting down at a table all by myself.

Ahead on the whiteboard, today's menu choices are posted:

STATION ONE
Pasta with meat sauce
Garlic bread

STATION TWO
Turkey or ham sandwich
Chicken and wild rice soup

STATION THREE
Spicy chicken sandwich
Seasoned potato crisps

Everything looks good as I hold my rabbit lunch of carrot and celery sticks. I should have brought money for hot lunch, but I thought bag lunch would be easier on the first day. One more bad idea.

"There's Gig." Isaac points.

On the other side of the cafeteria at the very end of the line, Gig's looking around.

"Over here," I holler.

He doesn't hear me.

"GIG!" I shout louder, but he still doesn't hear me.

"Keep it down," Mr. Tieg, the gym teacher, who's one of the lunch monitors, says sharply.

"Save my spot," I tell Isaac and walk across the cafeteria to Gig.

He finally sees me and rushes over.

"We're up by the front in this line."

"I sat for ten minutes in the wrong class last period before I figured out I wasn't in reading lab."

"What's reading lab?"

"Some loser class for people who don't like to read."

"Hey, no cutting," the girl with glasses from my bus says.

"I was already here." We squeeze in.

"We were saving their spot," Diego says.

"Thanks, San." Gig slaps Diego's hand.

"You can't save spots." The girl puts her hands on her hips.

"On the first day you can." I try to sound like I know what I'm doing.

24

"I'm getting pasta with meat sauce." Gig ignores the girl. "And a sandwich a la carte, too."

"What's a la carte?" I ask.

"They've got all kinds of things like french fries, onion rings, pizza, nachos and cheese. You've got to have a slip from your mom or dad, though, saying you can use your lunch account for a la carte."

I smell the garlic bread and know my lunch isn't going to be enough. I wish I had my sandwich back, the one that got stomped to bits on the bus floor.

We pick a table in back and I set out my carrot and celery sticks.

"That's all you've got, Nork?" Gig is horrified.

"Yes, and quit calling me Nork." I explain about the bus.

"That wouldn't have happened if I was there," he says.

I don't know what Gig would have done, but he's probably right. He would have thought of something.

I stare at Isaac's soup. "I'm going to eat hot lunch tomorrow."

"I told you lunch was going to be the best thing about middle school," Gig says.

"Have some of this." Isaac slides his soup across. "I don't want all of it."

"Thanks." I dig in.

"You can have this, Nork." Gig rips his garlic bread in half.

"I'm not Nork."

"Here." Diego hands me three apple slices.

"Thanks." I spread everything in front of me. These guys don't give up food very often.

"Excuse me, gentlemen." A man with a shaved head and tiny glasses comes over. "I'm Mr. Price, one of the counselors." Standing behind him is a dark-haired kid who seems totally lost. Mr. Price waves him forward. "This is Manny. He's new to the district and doesn't know anybody. Can he sit with you today?"

"Sure." Isaac slides over.

"Thank you, gentlemen," Mr. Price says.

"No problem." I sure hope he's not going to call us gentlemen every time he talks to us.

Manny sits down with his spicy chicken sandwich. That looks good, too.

"You're in sixth grade?" I ask, which is pretty stupid since this is the sixth-grade lunch period.

"Yes." He takes a small bite of his sandwich.

Diego asks him something in Spanish, and Manny responds with a long answer. He seems relieved to speak Spanish so Diego keeps asking him questions and he keeps talking.

I turn to Isaac and Gig. "Diego hasn't gotten his physical yet."

"What? Practice starts today." Isaac wipes his mouth with his hand.

"I know. He says his mom doesn't want him playing football."

"Maybe San's afraid," Gig says.

"I am not," Diego says loudly.

"Then where's your physical?" Gig challenges.

"I'm working on it."

"Yeah, right." Gig picks up some pasta that's fallen on his pants and eats it.

"Do you play football, Manny?" Isaac asks.

"He plays soccer," Diego says. "I told him he's got to get a physical if he wants to play in the Suburban Athletic League."

I take another bite of garlic bread. Diego's a soccer star. Maybe it's not his mom at all. Maybe he's the one who doesn't want to play football with us.

CHAPTER 5

*I*n advisory, Ms. Marcus announces that because she's such a warmhearted and caring human being and because it's such a beautiful day, we're going outside.

We all cheer. It's like having after-lunch recess back in elementary school. I loved recess, and not having it every day is going to be one of the worst things about middle school.

"In order to do this, however, we need you to proceed extra-quietly through the halls." Ms. Marcus holds a finger to her lips. "If you don't, we will never go outside for advisory again."

This gets everybody's attention and we tiptoe down the hall like little elves.

"Not bad, but there's still room for improvement." Ms. Marcus winks as she sets a mesh bag on the ground when we're outside. "We've got some balls and jump ropes here. You've got thirteen minutes."

A big guy grabs the football and he looks familiar. I try to remember where I've seen him before as a couple of his friends trail after him.

"Can I play with you?" Trenton asks.

"Get lost, loser." The guy turns his back on him.

I recognize him. He's the jerk from the Jaguars who pitched underhand to Sydney last spring.

I wish Isaac, Gig, and Diego were out here. They must have advisory teachers who aren't warmhearted human beings like Ms. Marcus. The only person I know in my advisory other than Trenton is Kelsey Neeley, Sydney's best friend. She's on the sidewalk with two other girls shaking their hips to keep hula hoops spinning, and I stare like I'm hypnotized.

I guess I do know one other person: Manny. The new kid is sitting by himself against the fence. Starting middle school is hard enough. Being new and not knowing anybody and not speaking good English must make it awful.

I pick a soccer ball out of the bag and walk over to the fence. I'd rather play football than soccer, but I'm not going to let those jerks tell me to get lost like they did to Trenton.

"Manny." I kick the ball to him and he jumps up. He weaves it around with his feet before he boots it back to me. I trap it the way I learned at soccer camp and send it back.

Manny tracks the ball down and sizzles a shot to me. He's got some skills. Trenton comes over and the three of us pass the ball around in a triangle. In middle school, people pay attention to who you hang out with. Trenton and Manny aren't going to be part of any popular crowd, but I don't care.

In the football game, they're playing two-hand touch. I'm as good as any of them. Next time I'm going to grab the football before anyone else does.

A pass is overthrown and the ball bounces our way. I pick it up and feel the leather as I grip the laces. I throw it as hard as I can at the jerk from the Jaguars, and the ball bounces in front of him and he jumps out of the way.

I turn my back on him and let him wonder whether I've got a bad arm or whether I did that on purpose.

After my afternoon classes of Spanish, where I become Julio since Jackson isn't Spanish sounding enough; science, where we review lab safety procedures since "safety is word one"; and American Studies, where we do a lot of first-day stuff, I'm eager for FACS. A-12 is in a different part of the building, and as soon as I leave the sixth-grade section, I notice the bigger seventh and eighth graders in the halls. I keep to the side and try to avoid eye contact.

A kid who's built like a weight lifter rumbles down the hall and I stay out of his way. Three boys behind me mutter, "Sixer, sixer, sixer," so I keep walking fast.

I'm in the A section, but I'm by the computer lab. A-2, A-6, these numbers feel random and I don't know which way to turn for A-12. Around the corner, Mr. Amodt, the librarian, is patrolling the hall.

"Think about signing up for READ Club tomorrow," he says to anyone who's listening. "READ stands for Read Every Awesome Day."

I stop and take out my map to let the older kids walk by.

"What are you looking for?" Mr. Amodt's got thick sideburns and strong arms.

"FACS."

"Straight down and take a right at the end of the hall. Listen for a sweet Southern accent, and you can't miss it."

I hurry along as the number of students in the hall thins. Longview is massive and it's hard to get from one side of the building to the other in the few minutes between periods.

Isaac's saved a seat for me in FACS.

"What's cooking?" I slide in next to him.

"I don't know but I hope we get to eat it."

"Me, too. Lunch seems like days ago."

The timer rings and the teacher, who's wearing capris and a blue floral top, checks the oven. "I'm Mrs. Randall and this is seventh-period FACS for the first trimester." She's got blond hair pulled back in a bun. "Look at your schedule and make sure y'all are in the right place."

I double-check my planner to make sure.

One of the football players from advisory raises his hand. "What's in the oven?"

"Cinnamon apple crisp," Mrs. Randall says. "If y'all pay close attention during the demo, you'll get to eat some."

I lean in toward Isaac. "This is going to be a good class."

"Please bring your chairs forward, ladies and gentlemen," Mrs. Randall says. "I'm going to demonstrate the proper procedure for making apple crisp so y'all will be able to do it for lab tomorrow."

Isaac raises his hand.

"Yes."

"Will we get to eat that, too?"

"If you don't burn it." She smiles.

I turn to Isaac, who's grinning. We're finally together, and this is the best class we could have to end the day.

CHAPTER 6

After Isaac's dad drops us off, we line up to get our football gear in the equipment room at Echo Park. While we wait, Gig complains loudly about school. "Whoever heard of homework on the first day?"

"Didn't you get time in advisory to do it?" Isaac asks.

"No," Gig says. "We spent the whole period organizing our stupid binders and writing assignments in our planners. I heard some classes got to go outside, but Mr. Corland said he doesn't believe in going outside on the first day like it's part of his religion or something. I can tell he's not going to be any fun. Boreland is more like it."

"What size waist do you have?" Coach Martineau asks. He's a short guy who's keeping the line moving.

"I don't know," I say.

"You should know your size." He eyes me and holds up a

set of girdle pads and two pairs of pants. "Put the pads in the practice pants and try them on. Keep moving."

I wrap my arms around everything and slide to the next station where Mr. Eberhart, the commissioner of the Suburban Athletic League, hands me a pair of shoulder pads. "These look good."

I move on to Coach Carson, who's a big guy with a goatee and tattooed arms. "Try this one on." He hands me a shiny white helmet.

I set my stuff on the ground and pull on the helmet, which scrunches up my ears.

Coach Carson raps me on the helmet with two hands. "That fits."

Next I go to Coach Tanglen, a tall, skinny guy who looks like he played basketball rather than football. He rips a piece of white tape off and sticks it to the front of my helmet.

"What's your last name?"

"Kennedy."

He writes it on the tape.

"What school do you go to?"

"Longview."

"Here's your practice jersey and your game jersey." He hands me a gray jersey and a red one with white trim with the number 83 on it. Red and white, the Longview colors. Even though we can't play for the school, we get the school colors. It's like we're in some in-between zone. We're part of middle school but not fully part of it.

Behind me, Gig and Isaac get their jerseys. I recognize some faces from Longview, but a lot I don't know. I check the line again. No Sydney. No trouble. I didn't think she was serious about coming out. Maybe she was messing around and wanted to see how I'd react. She can be weird that way. You never know what she's up to.

Gig, who's holding jersey number 43, and Isaac, who's number 11, walk over to the benches and I follow.

"No San," Gig says.

"What?" I jam my kneepad in my practice pants.

"No Diego." Isaac points to my pad. "That's upside down."

"He said he'd get his physical today." I adjust the kneepad.

"He's not going to play football," Gig says. "The soccer players are recruiting him, and he'll cave to their pressure.

"No, he won't." I yank on my girdle pads, which feel snug around my hips.

"How do you know?" Gig asks.

"He promised to play." I pull my tight pants over my pads, and it feels like sliding into a new skin.

Isaac yanks his belt tight. "That doesn't mean he will."

"After we all went to that stupid soccer camp," Gig says.

"Give him a chance." I swing my shoulder pads over my gray Under Armour shirt and immediately feel bigger and stronger. Why am I defending Diego? I don't think we're ever going to see him on the football field, either.

Coach Martineau leads us through our opening exercises. After sitting all afternoon in school, it feels good to be outside. I breathe in the warm air as I stand and cross my right leg over my left, lean down, and count with everybody to ten.

We switch to left leg over right and count that out.

"I can't hear you," Coach says.

"ONE, TWO, THREE," we shout.

Coach leads us in jumping jacks and more stretching. The whole time, I wish we could start playing. I'm ready to smash somebody.

"Gut busters," Coach calls as we all lie on our backs and raise our feet six inches off the ground. I hate these as my stomach muscles tighten.

"Three inches," Coach calls, and that's even worse.

"One inch."

When we finally finish, Coach makes us run two laps

around the field. "We need to get you in shape," he says. "Some of you have been spending too much time on video games and TV."

Gig, Isaac, and I run together. Some of the big linemen are already huffing and puffing. That's not a good sign. The three of us keep an even pace until the end when Gig sprints out in front. I run as I hard as I can but finish behind Isaac and him.

When everybody has dragged in, Coach Martineau has us take a knee in front of him. "We're going to run some drills so we can get an idea what you can do. We're not going to do any hitting today, though."

"Boooooo!" we complain.

"Listen, not all of you remembered your protective cups and I can see some of you don't even have mouth guards," he says. "I don't want anybody losing teeth or something even more valuable on the first day of practice. Make sure you bring your cups and mouth guards tomorrow and then we'll hit."

"Yeahhh!" we all cheer.

"We've got a lot of boys out this year," Coach says. "One of the goals in sixth-grade football is to give everybody a chance. To do this, we have offensive players and defensive players. All the coaches in the league have agreed that we're not going to have anybody going both ways. So think about it and decide what you want to play."

"I already know," Gig says. "Running back on offense."

"Quarterback." Isaac turns to me.

"I'm not sure." Last year in fifth-grade football, lots of us played both ways. I hate having to choose.

Chapter 7

While we're waiting to be picked up from practice, I listen to a voice mail from Mom. "Jackson, call me right away. I have great news."

I put my phone back in my bag. I'm not going to call her now. I've got a bad feeling that her definition of great news and mine aren't the same.

When Dad pulls up in the Subaru, I get in front and Gig and Isaac climb in back on either side of Quinn, my seven-year-old brother.

"How was the first day of middle school?" Dad asks.

"Fine." I roll down my window to get some fresh air among our sweaty bodies.

"Too much homework," Gig says.

"How about football practice?" Dad asks.

"Okay," I say, "but we didn't do any hitting."

"Tomorrow," Gig says. "Full contact."

"Full contact what?" Quinn asks.

"You get to smash into people." I put my helmet on the floor and wipe my face with my jersey.

"How's your dad doing, Gig?" Dad looks up in the rear-view mirror.

"Okay," Gig says quickly.

"He's in Afghanistan now?"

"Yeah." Gig stares out the window.

I can tell he doesn't want to talk about it, so I ask Isaac about where he catches the bus.

"Why are you asking about *my* stop?" he says.

"Because I hate mine."

When we get home I listen to Mom's voice mail again in my bedroom and try to figure out from her tone what the news is. Maybe it's about finding a place to live. She's been looking at a lot of houses in the past week. I call her back.

"Jackson, how was your first day?"

"Fine." I slide some clothes away and sit down on my bed.

"Really?"

"Yeah, it was fine." I lie back.

"I've got some great news."

"What?" I stare at the track of a jagged crack on the ceiling.

"I talked with Ted and he said he can move his office to the basement and that will allow you to have your own bedroom. I know that's important to you."

I don't say anything. I don't want to move into Mom's boyfriend's house.

"Heather and Haley come every other weekend, so most of the time you and Quinn will have plenty of space. When they are there, we'll work it out. They're such cooperative girls."

I still don't say anything.

"What do you think?" Mom says.

"I thought we were going to get our own place."

"I did, too. I've looked and looked. There isn't anything close to what we're accustomed to in our price range. There aren't many high quality rentals at reasonable prices, and there's no way we're living in some of the dumps I saw."

"Something smaller would have been okay. If it was ours."

"This is going to be ours, Jackson. You'll have your own room. Ted is making a generous offer and it's important to be grateful. Trust me, this is going to work out fine."

Yeah, right. I close my eyes and listen to her go on about how wonderful it will be.

———

*I*n the kitchen, Dad's sizzling hamburger in a frying pan, and it smells so good my mouth is watering.

"What are we having?"

"Tacos."

"I'm starving."

"How did your first day really go?" Dad turns the burner down.

"Fine." I sneak some cheese from the bowl on the counter.

"I had my first day of second grade today." Quinn looks up from his Legos. "Ms. Q is my teacher and she's nice. Well, sometimes she's not so nice, but that's only when people are talking and she has to clap her hands three times to get everybody's attention." He claps to demonstrate.

"Ms. Q?"

"Ms. Quanbeck," Dad says. "She's new this year."

"And we have activity stations and when we get free time we can go to any station we want, and Ms. Q has lots of books, and if we get our work done, we can take one and read it while the other kids are finishing their work."

"Great." I try to remember if I was ever that excited about school. If so, it was a long time ago.

"Wash your hands," Dad says. "We're ready."

Quinn and I rush to the bathroom, squirt some soap, wash it off, and hurry back.

"How were your classes?" Dad passes me taco shells and the bowl of hamburger at the kitchen table.

"Fine."

"How about your teachers?"

"Fine." I spoon salsa over the hamburger.

"And the bus?"

"I'm getting up earlier tomorrow." I scoop a big spoonful of cheddar cheese. "I'm going to walk over to Isaac's stop and get on there. I also want to eat hot lunch at school, so I need some money for that."

"Okay. Anything else bugging you?"

"Nope." I shake my head. I'm not going to tell Dad about moving to Ted's house yet. That's Mom's decision, and even though I don't like it, there's not a thing I can do about it.

CHAPTER 8

The next morning I leave the house extra early to go over to Isaac's bus stop. He's texting me while I'm walking so I know he's on his way, too. It's cooler this morning and there's a hint of fall in the air.

At the stop, Isaac waves me over. The gigantic guy from the back of the bus is standing off by himself texting and listening to his iPod at the same time. He sets his phone down on the brick wall while he searches through his backpack. Isaac shows me YouTube videos of crazy bike accidents on his phone. It's not supposed to be funny when people crash, but it's hard not to laugh.

When the bus arrives, the gigantic guy starts forward and I point to his phone. He turns around to grab it, but he doesn't even say thanks. He just plows ahead to the back of the bus.

I'm relieved to see plenty of open seats in the middle. I keep my head down, pick one, and slide all the way against the window. I want to turn around to see what Sunglasses and Spike Head are doing, but I don't want to call attention to myself, either. The best thing to do is to look straight ahead and hope they find another victim.

Isaac yawns and I do, too. I got up twenty minutes earlier today, and I don't have that first day of school excitement. Still, that's a small price to pay for not being in the back of the bus and having eighth graders eat my lunch.

At school, I hurry through the seventh-grade section trying to avoid any trouble and get to homeroom early. Sydney is already there and I walk over to her table. "What sport did you decide on?"

"Volleyball. Kelsey begged me."

"Good." I spin a pencil in my hand.

"What?"

"I think you'll be good." I'm glad she's not playing football with us, and I don't want to say anything that might cause her to change her mind. Then I remember what else I wanted to ask her. "How's your dad doing?"

"Okay. He's stationed on a base outside Kabul. We got to

talk to him last night on Skype. He looked exhausted, but he was still making jokes. It was really good to see him."

"You saw him?"

"Yeah, the computer's got a webcam. Didn't Gig tell you about it?"

"No." Gig hasn't talked much about his dad since he found out he was going to Afghanistan last spring.

"**D**id you get your physical last night?" I ask Diego as he waits for me at my locker before gym.

"I couldn't. My brother called but the clinic said they were full."

"But you're still going to get it, right?" I spin my combination.

"We're going to try again today."

My locker jams again and Diego yanks on the corner with both hands while I pull on the handle until we finally get it open.

"Hey, what's going on?" Ms. Tremont rushes over like she's uncovered a crime.

"My locker doesn't work."

"Well, you shouldn't be pulling on it like that."

"That's the only way I can get it open."

"We'll see if we can get it fixed." She writes down my name and locker number in her notebook.

I throw my stuff in and we head to gym.

"You want to play football, right?" I say to Diego.

"I guess."

"You don't sound sure."

"My mom thinks it's violent."

"It's not violent. It's fun."

Diego steps aside to avoid a charging eighth grader. "I've never played. I don't know if I'd be any good."

"Trust me. You're going to be good."

*I*n advisory we work on organizing our planners and binders. It's pretty simple, but some kids keep making mistakes.

"I've got a sign-up sheet for READ Club up here," Ms. Marcus says. "Read Every Awesome Day. Mr. Amodt is recruiting new members this year. You meet twice a month over lunch and advisory, and you get extra privileges like being able to check out as many books as you want and getting to read books before they are released to the public."

Three girls put their names down and Kelsey goes up.

"That's four," Ms. Marcus says. "Let's have a few more."

Two more girls go up to sign the sheet.

"Look who has signed up," Ms. Marcus says. "Mr. Amodt specifically told me he wanted more boys this year. We need at least one boy to sign up."

I examine scratch marks on the table. I don't need one more thing to do.

"Come on," Kelsey says. "One of you chickens sign up."

"I'll sweeten the offer." Ms. Marcus winks. "If we get a boy on the list, we'll go outside for the rest of advisory today."

A number of boys have their heads down.

"Do it, Jackson," Kelsey whispers.

"Oh, okay." I stand up and everybody cheers. Not for me, but for going outside.

Manny is kicking the soccer ball around with Trenton and a couple of other guys, but that's not what I want to do. I walk over to the football game, and the jerk from baseball notices me.

"What do you want?" he says.

"I want to play."

"You any good?" he snarls.

"Yeah, I can play."

"Okay," he says. "You're on defense."

I jog over to the other side of the ball and split out wide to cover a short guy chewing bubble gum. He doesn't look that good.

"Hut, hut." The Jerk, who's playing quarterback, drops back.

Bubble Gum races off the line and cuts in. He's faster than I expected and I'm a step slow keeping up. Bubble Gum turns to go deep and has me beat, but the Jerk over-throws him.

I jog back to the line of scrimmage. Close call. I almost gave up a touchdown on my first play.

"Let's go." One of my teammates claps.

On second down, Bubble Gum goes down and out and the Jerk fakes the pass. Bubble Gum turns upfield and I shadow him. He extends his arm and I turn around just in time to stick my hand out and knock the ball away.

On third and ten, the Jerk rolls out and Bubble Gum fakes inside and cuts for the sideline. I guess they'll go for the quick pass for the first down so I jump in front just as the ball is released. I grab it and take off running. I fake to the inside and the Jerk steps that way and I cut back and beat him outside.

"Touchdown," my teammates cheer.

I jog back holding the ball up. "Seven to nothing. We're up." I flip it to the Jerk who stares at me.

I line up at my position on defense. I love this game.

"**W**e're going to start the year with a bang." Mr. Lisicky, my American Studies teacher, punches his fist against his hand. "The Boston Massacre, Paul Revere's Ride, Lexington, Concord, Valley Forge, Yorktown. We're going to learn about the founding of this nation, the American Revolution." He paces back and forth in the front of the room. "You will find out that Samuel Adams was not a beer, but a patriot, and that the patriots were not a football team, but people who risked everything, including their lives, for an idea."

I stare out the window and wish the clock could speed forward. I'd like to be outside playing football right now not sitting in class listening to another boring teacher.

"For tomorrow, you get to read chapter one." Mr. Lisicky acts like he's giving us an exciting opportunity. "And I want you all to do a bit of research on one person, Crispus Attucks." He writes the name on the whiteboard and we all copy it down. "Find out who he was and why he's important."

Great. Just great. More homework.

I replay my interception while Mr. Lisicky chatters on about the Stamp Act. It feels so good to step in front of a receiver when he thinks he's going to catch the ball and snatch it out of the air and take it the other way for a touchdown. Even better when the quarterback is the Jerk.

I like playing both offense and defense and wish I didn't have to choose. But Isaac and Gig are on offense and want me there. I should stick with them.

CHAPTER 9

After a long afternoon, I'm ready to make some apple crisp in FACS. Better yet, I'm ready to eat apple crisp.

But before we can do that, Mrs. Randall splits us up into food lab groups. Of course I get separated from Isaac and put in a group with nobody I know: one boy and two girls. Why can't we choose our own groups?

"Listen closely," Mrs. Randall says. "I'm passing out a gold sheet listing four jobs for four upcoming food labs. Write down your name for a different job for each lab in order to experience different responsibilities."

The smell of apples and cinnamon is making me hungry, and I wish we could get started. The girl across from me has dangly orange earrings and cowboy boots that match, and she's taken charge of our group. She's writing everybody's names in the boxes and telling us what to do.

"Here's a green sheet," Mrs. Randall says. "These are the eight steps we use to make mouth-watering apple crisp. I want y'all to sign up to be responsible for two steps."

The bossy girl writes her name down for two tasks and passes the sheet to the boy on her left. By the time it gets all the way around to me, only two steps are left.

Step 5: Mix dry ingredients with a pastry blender until crumbly.

Step 6: Pour sliced apples into an eight-by-eight pan.

I'm disappointed I couldn't choose Step 8, which is to place the apple crisp in the oven and remove it after twenty minutes. Bossy Boots took that for herself.

"All ready?" Mrs. Randall asks.

"Yes, ma'am," we respond. Mrs. Randall is from Alabama and politeness is super important to her.

Our group moves over to Kitchen Three and since I don't have any jobs right away I search for Isaac. He's busy peeling apples in Kitchen One and a girl with a long ponytail is laughing at something he said.

The other boy in our group turns on the oven and sprays the baking pan. After that he takes out a notebook and draws pictures of aliens and spaceships. Bossy Boots is peeling apples, and I stand next to the other girl, who's tall with reddish brown hair. She's wearing a purple long-sleeved T-shirt that says GUESS WHAT in shiny letters.

"Want to help?" She points to our ingredients list.

"Okay." I pass her the oats and get a whiff of her shampoo, which smells like pineapple.

"What's your name?" she asks.

"Jackson." I hand her brown sugar.

"I've got a cousin named Jackson." She measures the ingredients neatly and pours them into the mixing bowl.

"What's yours?"

"Ruby." She holds out her hand like she's going to offer it, but it's got butter on it so she just raises it. "In Spanish class, I'm Reyna," she says.

"I'm Julio."

"*Hola*, Julio."

"*Hola*, Reyna." I continue to hand her ingredients as we talk. Sometimes around girls I get tongue-tied and don't know what to say, but Ruby's different. She asks me questions and makes talking easy. I look at the front of her T-shirt again. "What am I supposed to guess?"

"Whatever you like."

At football practice, Coach Tanglen walks among us as we do thirty push-ups. "Football players need to be strong," he says. "Count it out."

"One, two, three." I dip my chest to the dry grass.

By the time I get to thirty, my arms are shaking and I'm not going down as low.

"We expect you to improve on these," Coach Tanglen says. "You need to build up your strength."

When everybody is finished, we sit on the ground.

"Those of you who want to play offense, go down with Coach Martineau. Those of you who want to play defense, stay here with me."

"Let's go, Nork." Gig pulls me up by my gray practice jersey.

"I'm not Nork." I tuck my jersey in.

"Then you have to think of a better name," Gig says.

"Let's see some hustle," Coach Martineau calls.

"Come on." Isaac gives me a push.

I run with Isaac and Gig, but I glance over my shoulder to see who stayed on defense with Coach Tanglen.

"Split up into three lines," Coach Martineau says. "Zig-zag drill." He demonstrates running ten yards one way, then ten yards the other in the shape of a Z.

That's easy, but we run one drill after another without touching a football. I look down at the defensive players who are covering each other one on one while Coach Tanglen throws long passes. That looks way more fun.

"Gather in," Coach Martineau says. "If you look down-field, you'll see we don't have the right ratio of offensive players to defensive players. We have two-thirds of you here while only one-third is down with Coach Tanglen." He sounds like my math teacher.

"Eventually we will even the percentages out," he says. "I know everybody wants to carry the ball and score touch-downs, but on a team we need people at all the different positions. Those of you who like playing defense, I want you to consider going down and joining Coach Tanglen."

I kind of want to go down there, but Gig and Isaac squeeze in behind me like they can read my mind. Tony Cerrato and Noah Hauser, who played baseball with us, run down.

"That's a start." Coach Martineau claps. "We'll need

some more of you to make the switch by Friday. You can do it on your own or we'll choose for you."

For the next drill, I'm at the end of the line with Gig. "I told you San wasn't going to show," he says.

"He's trying to get his physical today." I untangle my chin-strap.

"Yeah, right."

"What makes you think you know everything Diego's going to do?"

"I know he's chicken to play football," Gig spits.

I step away from him and join the line with Isaac. I wish Diego would come out. If he doesn't, I'm going to feel like a nork for saying he would.

CHAPTER 10

"**Y**our grandpa wants to take us out for pizza at Green Mill to celebrate the first week of school," Dad announces when I get home.

"Pizza, pizza!" Quinn chants as we walk to the car.

"What kind of pizza do you want?" Dad unlocks the doors.

"Pepperoni." I climb in front.

"Me, too," Quinn joins in.

"G-Man will probably choose something strange." I buckle my seat belt. *G-Man*'s what Quinn and I call Grandpa because he says he's too young to be called Grandpa.

When we get to Green Mill, G-Man's already staked out a booth in back.

"How's the big second grader?" G-Man gives Quinn a fake punch.

"Great," Quinn says and starts telling G-Man about Ms. Q.

"Miscue?" G-Man says. "Like a mistake?"

"No, Ms. Q." Dad draws the letter on his place mat. "Short for Quanbeck."

"Why doesn't she use Quanbeck?" G-Man asks.

"Ms. Q. is easier," Quinn says.

"Aye, yay, yay." G-Man rubs his hair. "My first-grade teacher was Miss Papadopoulos and my second-grade one was Mrs. Schlossmacher. We didn't have any trouble saying their names."

Quinn ignores him and describes decorating his writer's notebook and writing whatever he wants to in it each day.

"And how about you, Jackson?" G-Man turns to me. "How's middle school?"

"Good." I pick up a menu even though I know what I want.

"Any problems?"

"My locker's junk."

"Tell them you need a decent one," G-Man says. "How are your classes?"

"Good."

"¿Hablas español?"

"*Sí.*" I hold my thumb and finger close together to indicate a little.

"*¿Quién es su maestra?*"

"What?"

"What's your teacher's name?"

"Señora O'Reilly."

G-Man bursts out laughing so loud that people at other tables turn to look. "O'Reilly, that's a fine Spanish name. You tell Señora O'Reilly that you're a Kennedy from County Cork and find out where her people come from. Tell her you are the descendant of Donovans, Sullivans, and O'Malleys and see if she's got any of those names in her background."

G-Man goes on about Irish immigration to the United States like he's an American Studies teacher. He's interested in all kinds of stuff that nobody else cares about.

The waitress comes to our booth and takes our order. Dad and G-Man have to split their pizza in half since Dad wants mushrooms and black olives and G-Man wants pineapple and anchovies. Even Dad, who likes all kinds of different foods, rolls his eyes at that.

"Pineapple and anchovies are a perfect combination of sweet and savory," G-Man tells the waitress. "They don't know what they're missing."

"Yes, we do," I say.

"And one large Caesar salad," Dad says. "These boys need some veggies."

I look over at Quinn and stick my tongue out and he laughs.

"How's football?" G-Man turns to me.

"Okay, but we've got to choose either offense or defense."

"That's tough," G-Man says. "I think you should choose defense."

"Ahhhemm." Dad clears his throat.

"What?" G-Man holds up his hands.

"That's Jackson's decision."

"I know it is," G-Man says. "I'm just stating my opinion."

When we get home, Dad asks me about homework the second we walk in.

"I've got research for American Studies, thirty minutes of reading for language arts, vocabulary for Spanish, and two pages of math problems."

"Better get started."

"Why do they have to give us so much?"

"You're in middle school now," Dad says, like that's some sort of news flash.

I don't feel like doing any of it. I'd rather sit and watch TV.

"I've got homework, too." Quinn stands next to me in the living room.

"What's your homework?" Dad asks.

"I've got to bring in something about my family." Quinn acts like this is a super-serious assignment.

"You could take some pictures in," Dad suggests.

"Somebody already did that," Quinn says. "I want something different, like if we had a dog I could take him."

"We don't have a dog," Dad says.

"I wish we did. A dog would be perfect."

"What about if you went online and printed the menu from Green Mill and told them what kind of pizza each person ordered tonight?" I say.

"Nah," Quinn says. "Besides I don't know what kind Mom would choose."

"She likes black olives and mushrooms, too."

"Jackson, why don't you sit down at the kitchen table and start with *your* homework. I'll work with Quinn."

"I was just trying to help."

"I know, but you've got your own work. What would you like to start with?"

"Nothing."

"If you can't finish your homework, we won't be able to go out on school nights in the future," Dad warns.

So I grab my backpack and take out my books. I'm drowning in homework already. Every teacher is giving us lots without realizing every other teacher is doing the same thing. It's too much. Dad doesn't understand that when I have so much, I don't want to sit down and start because once I do, it's going to take forever to finish.

I want to zone out with the TV, not find out who some random guy named Crispus Attucks was.

CHAPTER 11

*T*he next morning I rest my head on my desk as Mr. Tedesco demonstrates how to correctly use a ruler in math class. He's got black hair, beady eyes, and looks like a crow. I wouldn't be shocked if he started cawing and flying around the room. Anyway we all know how to use a ruler. We're in sixth grade, not second.

I'm tired from staying up late doing homework. Between school, football, and homework, I'm not going to have much time for myself. I knew we'd have more homework in middle school, but I didn't think it would be this much.

Mr. Tedesco emphasizes measuring twice to be sure. He's also the eighth-grade football coach, and since I want to play in two years, I need to look awake. I don't know if he'll remember me then, but I sit up and pretend to be interested in rulers.

When the bell rings, I rush out of the room and down the

hall to the drinking fountain. Next to it is the Wall of Heroes and straight in front of me is a new picture of Gig's dad.

PFC ROBERT MILROY

FATHER OF SYDNEY AND SPENCER MILROY

ARMY NATIONAL GUARD

CURRENTLY SERVING IN AFGHANISTAN

I've known Gig's dad for years and it's strange to see a picture of him all dressed up in his uniform. I move closer to the picture. That's not the way he usually looks when he's smoking a cigar at their kitchen table.

On my way to language arts, I run into Gig outside of Mr. Tedesco's room. "Nice picture of your dad."

"Where?"

"On the Wall of Heroes."

"She didn't," Gig says angrily. "I told her not to." He turns away and heads down the hall.

"Gig!" I holler. "You're going to be late."

Part of me wants to chase after him to see what he's doing, but I don't want to get another late slip, either. Three of those and you get detention, which means missing football practice. Missing football practice means not starting.

"Get to class," Mr. Norquist, the assistant principal, who's patrolling the halls, calls out and I hurry along.

In language arts, Ms. Tremont checks our reading logs and I'm glad I made sure to write mine down.

Five minutes reading menu at Green Mill
Ten minutes reading stats at nfl.com
Fifteen minutes at guinnessworldrecords.com

The last one was the best since I found out the shortest time to eat a whole pizza (under two minutes) and the most cockroaches eaten in one minute (thirty-six). Ms. Tremont talks about the wealth of good books written for students our age, but I have a hard time concentrating. I keep thinking about Gig and why he stormed off.

In American Studies, Mr. Lisicky acts like we're going to be interested in something that happened over two hundred years ago.

"Who was Crispus Attucks?"

The smart kids raise their hands, but Mr. Lisicky ignores them. "Jackson."

"What?"

"Who was Crispus Attucks?"

"He was the first person killed in the Boston Massacre." I'm glad that I looked it up.

"That's right," Mr. Lisicky says, "but who was Crispus Attucks?"

"He was a slave who ran away from his master and worked on whaling ships."

"That's right," Mr. Lisicky says. "What do we know about his parents?"

I raise my hand again because I know this answer, too.

"Yes, Jackson."

"His dad was born in Africa and brought to America as a slave and his mom was an Indian."

"Good work." Mr. Lisicky nods. He calls on other people, and unlike some teachers who only call on kids whose hands are in the air, Mr. Lisicky calls on anybody. I'm going to have to make sure I remember to do my homework in here.

"By 1770, many Boston citizens resented the presence of British soldiers in their city." Mr. Lisicky moves his hands while he talks. "On the evening of March 5, 1770, a soldier hit a boy who had accused an officer of not paying a bill. A mob gathered and people started throwing sticks, snowballs, and chunks of ice at the soldiers. A British officer called out men of the Twenty-ninth Regiment, and Crispus Attucks and other sailors came up from the docks to confront the soldiers. Mr. Attucks was at the front of the group, and in the confusion, someone yelled, 'Fire!' Two bullets pierced his chest."

Mr. Lisicky tells the story like he was there. "Crispus Attucks was the first person to give his life for the cause of American independence, a man who had been born into slavery and whose father was African and whose mother was a Native American. He received a hero's burial along with four comrades and became a symbol for those colonists who desired freedom."

I've never been very interested in stuff that happened long ago, but Mr. Lisicky makes it feel different, more real.

"I've got another name for you." He goes to the board. "For tomorrow, find out who Henry Knox was and what he did in 1776."

At football practice, we do our usual exercises and laps to start the practice. When we split into offense and defense, Gig, Isaac, and I go with the group with Coach Martineau.

"We're going to make decisions on positions the next couple of days," Coach announces. "We've got to decide so we can get a basic offense in. We've got our first game against the Hawks coming up next week."

I stand next to Isaac as Coach talks. Gig's kneeling down picking at the grass. He's not joking around and acting like his usual self.

"Line up over here if you want to play quarterback," Coach calls out.

Isaac walks over with two guys I don't know.

"Running backs, here."

Gig gets up slowly and joins a big group.

"Receivers, here."

I shuffle over with a bunch of others.

"Linemen, go with Coach Carson."

Eight big guys stand up. Carson is a college student who used to go to school here and who's volunteering with the football team. He's so huge, he must be a former lineman.

I stand with the group around Coach Martineau. Most people want to touch the ball and score points. The linemen, who do all the dirty work, get a lot less attention and that's why fewer people go out for those positions.

Downfield Coach Tanglen has the defensive players backpedaling as fast as they can. One of the defensive linemen falls over and everybody laughs.

"Get back up." Coach claps. "Quick feet, quick feet. We want quick feet on defense."

I follow Coach Martineau as he separates us into three groups. I'm good at backpedaling and I've got quick feet.

Coach positions each of three lines with a different quarterback and I'm lucky to be with Isaac.

"Hut, hut," he calls and drops back. He fires a tight spiral to the first receiver who stretches out his hands to make a good grab.

I watch the two other quarterbacks. Neither one is as good as Isaac. He's got the starting quarterback spot nailed down.

My turn comes and I run as fast as I can. Isaac launches a rocket, but the ball is behind me. I turn and get my hands on it, but the ball bounces off. I chase down the rolling football while Coach Martineau watches.

"Grab it and tuck it away," he says.

I throw the ball in and jog back.

"Catch the ball," Isaac says. "You're making me look bad."

"Put it on target."

"You got your hands on it. Hang on!"

In the other line, Gig makes a fantastic grab of a ball that's overthrown. He's got good hands and great speed. He's a lock to start at running back.

Quincy, another receiver who's fast, races down the field. Isaac throws as far as he can and Quincy turns it up into another gear and races under it. He's a star. Lots of these guys are.

I don't know that I'm going to beat them out for a starting spot. I kick at the patch of dirt in front of me. I might not get to play on offense.

CHAPTER 12

After practice, Mom and Quinn pick me up in the mini-van. We're with Mom Thursday through Sunday, and then Dad picks us up, and we stay with him until Thursday morning. Half and half. We've done it this way for a couple of years now.

Mom gives me a kiss when I get in. I wish she wouldn't do that stuff when other kids are around.

"How is everything at middle school?"

"Fine."

"Really?" She waits until I'm buckled in to turn the car on.

"Yeah, it's fine. The lunches are good and we get to make things to eat in FACS."

"How are the classes where you don't eat?"

"They're fine, too." I roll down my window.

"Do you have homework tonight?"

"A little."

"Your dad said you had a lot last night."

"We stayed inside at advisory today and I got most of it done."

"I don't have any homework tonight, either," Quinn says from the backseat. He starts telling Mom about how Connor brought a guinea pig for show-and-tell and how all the kids loved it and how much fun pets are. I'm glad he's such a blabbermouth since I don't feel like talking about school now.

"We're going to stop at Subway and pick up some sandwiches," Mom says. "We'll get them to go and eat at the house."

"Yeah, Subway," Quinn cheers.

"Does that sound good to you, Jackson?"

"Yeah, fine." Subway's okay, but I was hoping for something better.

"I heard a disturbing report on *All Things Considered*." Mom looks at me when we get to a stop sign.

"What?"

"A number of former professional athletes are showing signs of brain trauma. Doctors are increasingly concerned about the long-term consequences of concussions."

I stare out the window. Not her now.

"Football's a dangerous game," she says. "Sometimes I wish you weren't playing it."

"I love football."

"I know," she says. "I wish you didn't love it so much."

At the house, cardboard boxes are spread out around the rooms. Some are partly packed. Some are packed, taped shut, and labeled.

"When are we moving?" I ask.

"Sunday," Quinn says excitedly.

I set my backpack down on the floor. How come he knows more about what's going on around here than I do?

"I told you we were moving in with Ted," Mom says.

"I didn't know it was so soon."

"Liz and Jeff are back from Italy next week. I want all our stuff out this weekend so I can get the house clean for them."

Mom goes into the kitchen and opens the fridge. "What do you want to drink?"

"Apple juice," I say.

"Me, too." Quinn opens his bread and eats a pickle slice.

I unwrap my turkey and cheese sandwich and look around at the boxes. This was never our house, just a place we were staying while Mom's friends were gone. Even so, it felt like home. I've never even seen Ted's house. There's no way that's going to feel like home.

After we eat, Mom and Quinn carry empty boxes to his room to pack. I open Mom's laptop on the dining room table to do my American Studies homework. Usually I don't like to do homework right away, but I'd rather do that than pack boxes and think about Ted and moving into his house.

I find Henry Knox on Wikipedia and it says he's an American bookseller from Boston. Why is Lisicky having us research some old guy who sold books?

I pull out my phone and see a text from Isaac asking what I'm doing.

Nothing, I text back.

He calls me right away.

"What's the matter with Gig?" he says.

"I don't know. Why?"

"He hardly said anything to me at practice even when I tried to talk with him. He got into an argument with Dante, one of the other running backs. He seems mad about something."

I tell Isaac about the picture and Gig getting angry.

"You need to talk to him," Isaac says.

"Why me?"

"He listens to you."

"He doesn't listen to anybody."

Isaac switches to talking about the team and how fast the receivers are and what good hands they have. "We've got some talent."

"Yeah." I tap my fingers on the table. Is he trying to tell me something?

Gig doesn't answer the first three times when I call him so I send a text telling him to answer his phone.

He finally calls me back. "What do you want?"

"To talk about football," I say. "What do you think of the team?"

"It's okay," he says. "I wish Coach Tanglen ran the offense. Coach Martineau is kind of boring. He spends too much time on drills."

"Yeah, I know what you mean."

"I've got to go," Gig says. "I've got a ton of homework and my mom is checking up on me."

I want to ask about what happened with Sydney and the

picture of his dad, but I can tell he doesn't want to talk about it. He doesn't seem to want to talk to any of us.

As I'm lying in bed, I realize I only have a few more nights in this house. That feels weird, especially since I can't picture where we're going. I try to imagine being at Ted's house. What's it going to be like to have Heather and Haley around? I've never been around girls like that.

I roll over on my back and feel wide awake. I didn't tell Gig anything about the move. I guess we both have secrets. I didn't tell Isaac, either. He kept talking about how talented the receivers are. Is he telling me I'm not good enough to start? I don't want to stand around on the sidelines and watch.

Right now my best chance to start is switching to defense. I don't care what Gig and Isaac think. I've got to do what's best for me.

CHAPTER 13

I hold Diego's feet as he whips off twenty sit-ups in gym class Friday morning. When we switch places, he counts for me.

"Elbows to knees," Mr. Tieg barks out.

"I thought gym was supposed to be fun," I whisper to Diego.

"It beats general music," he says.

"Not by much."

"Listen up," Mr. Tieg says. "We're going outside for our first timed run of the trimester. I want you to run as hard as you can twice around the track, a half mile."

"I wish we'd play some games," I say as we walk out together.

"A half mile isn't long." Diego wipes his face on his T-shirt.

"What's going on with your physical?" I'm getting tired of asking about it.

"I got it last night." Diego holds the door open for me.

"You did? You're coming to football practice today?" The fresh air feels good.

"No." He shakes his head slowly.

"Why not?"

"My mom won't sign the permission form. I told you she wouldn't. She doesn't want me getting hurt."

"You could get hurt riding your bike to school or walking down the hall. She can't make sure that you never get hurt." I kick a rock that slides across the asphalt. "Why don't you get your dad to sign it?"

"He wants me to play soccer."

"Why don't you tell them it's for soccer and come out for football?"

Diego looks at me like I'm crazy. "That's a really bad idea."

"We're picking positions at practice. You're running out of time."

At lunch I sit with Gig and Isaac at our regular table. Across the way, Ruby demonstrates dance moves and her friends all laugh.

"Look, they're trying to recruit San." Gig points at Diego, who's talking to Manny and some soccer players.

"San's not a good nickname for Diego." Isaac squeezes honey onto his peanut butter sandwich.

"Come up with something better, Ike," Gig says. "He needs a nickname."

"How about Charger?" Isaac says. "San Diego Charger."

"No, sounds like a horse." I dip a chicken nugget in barbeque sauce. "How about Padre? San Diego Padre."

"Now you're thinking, Nork." Gig slaps me on the back. "Padre is great."

"Quit calling me Nork."

"Think of something better then." Gig bites into his cheeseburger. I'm glad he's in a better mood today.

"What about Jax with an *x*?" Isaac says.

"Too lame, Ike." Gig shakes his head.

"What about JK?" I rub some sauce off my chin.

"Just kidding?" Gig says. "That's lame, too."

"In Spanish class, I'm Julio."

"I like Julio," Isaac says.

"I'll be Julio then," I say strongly.

"It's kind of weak." Gig shrugs his shoulders. "You can be Julio if you want. But you still look norky."

"Shut up." I give him a shove.

Mr. Norquist is talking to Mr. Tieg and they both start walking to our table. Did they see that?

"Which one of you is Spencer Milroy?" Norquist says in his gruff voice.

"Gig, not Spencer," Gig responds.

"You're Milroy?"

Gig nods and pops another Tater Tot in his mouth.

"Have you been taking down pictures of servicemen from the Wall of Heroes?"

"My dad's picture," Gig says. "It wasn't supposed to be there."

"Come with me right now," Norquist commands.

Gig gets up and reaches for a handful of Tater Tots. For someone who loves food, leaving his lunch behind might be worse than going off with the assistant principal.

"Why did he take the picture down?" Isaac grabs Gig's food.

"Sydney put it up."

"Oh." He knows how much the two of them fight. "Still that's stupid to get Norquist involved."

*I*n American Studies, I'm glad when Mr. Lisicky calls on other people because I didn't write much down about the bookseller guy.

"Henry Knox was present at the Boston Massacre," a girl says.

"He became the first secretary of war for the United States," a boy says. "Both Fort Knox and Knoxville are named after him."

"But what did he do in 1776?" Mr. Lisicky asks.

"He took some cannons from Fort Ticonderoga and brought them to Boston," one of the smart girls says.

"SOME CANNONS?" Mr. Lisicky shouts. "They pulled fifty-eight cannons that weighed over sixty tons for three hundred miles in the middle of the winter from upstate New York to Boston! Oxen hauled them across the frozen Hudson River and over the Berkshire Mountains." He waves his hands around. "One of the oxen drivers was John Becker and guess how old he was?"

Nobody raises a hand.

"John Becker was twelve. Not much older than you."

Twelve? I check my notes, which don't have any of this.

"Henry Knox was twenty-five and his brother William was nineteen, and when all these cannons appeared on Dorchester Heights in Boston on the morning of March 5, 1776, the British couldn't believe it. They didn't think that anybody could pull off such an extraordinary feat. Their army and fleet fled Boston, giving the Americans a significant victory." Mr Lisicky paces back and forth in the front of the room and sounds like he wishes we all could have been there. "What was Henry Knox's job?"

I raise my hand.

"Jackson."

"He was a bookseller."

"Yes, he began working in a bookstore after his father died when he was about your age. He had to drop out of school to help earn money for his family, but he didn't stop learning. He read books about all kinds of things including cannons, mortars, and transportation, and like many of the American patriots, he was largely self-educated, meaning he read to learn, not because he had to for school. Reading allowed him to envision this idea of bringing cannons across the mountains in the middle of winter to force the British army, the most powerful in the world, to retreat from Boston."

Mr. Lisicky looks around at each of us. "Never underestimate what you can learn from reading."

"**W**hat happened with Norquist?" I ask Gig at practice as I tie my laces tight.

"He said I'd committed a serious offense, a violation of Longview rules and school spirit. He said I desecrated a shrine to American heroes."

"Wow."

"I tried to explain about Sydney, but he didn't listen. He totally took her side and said she's entitled to place a picture of her father on the Wall of Heroes and everybody in the school must respect it. He said it didn't matter what I felt about it."

"That's not fair." I pull on my elbow pad. "He's your dad, too."

"I don't want everybody knowing my business and asking me about it or treating me like somebody to feel sorry for because my dad is gone."

"What's Norquist going to do?"

"He threatened to suspend me for three days and called up Ms. Monihan. I didn't even know she was my counselor, but she came in and told Norquist that I'm in a challenging situation and that different family members handle these things differently. She said it wasn't fair to expect me to do things the same way Sydney does."

"You've been saying that for years."

"Yeah, Ms. Monihan calmed Norquist down and recommended I go to a group she leads for family members of service personnel. Norquist wanted me to go to a conflict management group, too, but she said one group was enough. They made me agree to do that in order to avoid the suspension."

"Good."

"I still don't want to go to some stinkin' group."

I lean forward to touch my toes as Isaac leads us in stretching. I can't believe we've finished the first week of middle school. It was a short week because we didn't have school on Monday, but it still went fast.

"Over here," Coach Martineau calls.

I pick up my helmet as we gather around the coaches. I meant to tell Gig and Isaac about deciding to switch to defense, but the time never seemed right.

"Offensive players stay here with me," Coach Martineau says. "Coach Tanglen still needs some more players on defense. Anybody interested in switching, go down with him."

I start walking that way with the defensive players.

"Where are you going?" Isaac grabs my jersey.

"I'm going to play defense."

"Why?"

"I've got a better chance of starting there." I back out of his grasp.

"You said you were playing offense," Gig says angrily. "What's the matter with you?"

"What's going on over there?" Coach Martineau asks.

"Nothing," Isaac says.

I run down to catch up with Coach Tanglen and the defensive players. Isaac and Gig don't understand. They're both so good that they'll start for sure on offense. Halfway down the field, though, I feel like I'm making a big mistake. The defensive players have been together for a couple of days. Maybe the positions are already set.

Maybe I won't start on defense either.

CHAPTER 14

"**K**ennedy." Coach Tanglen reads the tape on my helmet. "Welcome to defense."

"Thanks." The other players stand around talking and joking with each other. They seem looser than the offensive players.

"Z drill to start with," Coach says. "Sportelli, demonstrate it for Kennedy."

Sam Sportelli, who I used to play baseball with, runs ten yards forward, stops, and backpedals ten yards making a Z pattern as he runs down the field. It's like the drill we did the other day except we run forward and then backward.

"Line up along the marker lines," Coach says.

We buckle our chinstraps and hustle out. I stand by Sam on the twenty-yard line.

"Go!" Coach barks.

I sprint forward to keep up with Sam, but when I switch to backpedal, my feet get tangled up, and I fall over on my butt.

"You move like an offensive player, Kennedy," Coach says. "Get back up. Quick feet. We need quick feet on defense."

I scramble back up and run out the rest of the drill, but I finish way behind everybody else including the big linemen.

"We're going to focus on pursuit angles today," Coach says. "Some of you are taking bad angles. That's why you're getting beat."

Coach crouches down like a linebacker and points to Tony. "Cerrato, pretend you're taking a pitch and running wide."

Tony lines up at running back opposite Coach.

"Hut, hut," Coach yells.

Tony holds his hands out, catches an imaginary ball, and runs hard. Coach springs out of his stance and rushes toward the sideline. He lowers his shoulder like he's going to clobber him, but at the last moment holds up.

"If you take too wide an angle, you're going to give up too many yards." He turns to us. "If your angle is too sharp, you're going to miss the tackle all together. That happened a couple of times yesterday. We need to take the right angle. It's all geometry, boys."

I've never thought of it that way before. I thought you just ran as hard as you could and tackled the guy with the ball.

"We'll work on this until it becomes second nature," Coach says. "In a game, we don't want you stopping to think about it, we want you to automatically take the best angle and make the tackle."

Coach splits us up into groups; half of us are ball carriers and half are tacklers.

"No hitting on this," Coach cautions.

I take out my mouth guard. Being able to hit was one of the main reasons I wanted to play defense.

Noah Hauser rushes wide and a big kid chases after him. He meets him at the sideline and gives Noah a shove. It's the Jerk.

"Good angle, Speros." Coach claps.

Speros jogs back to the end of the line. I hated him in baseball, but now he's my teammate. That feels really strange.

Sam lines up as the next ball carrier and I take my position on defense.

"Hut, hut." Sam races around the side and he's faster than

I expected. I lunge but end up grabbing air as he skitters down the field.

"Take the right angle, Kennedy," Coach warns. "Do it again."

I hurry back and line up. These guys have been practicing together and know what Coach expects. They've got a huge head start on me.

Friday night and Saturday morning are packing times with Mom.

"Aren't these great boxes?" She hands me a white box with holes on the side for handles. "Ted can get all we need at his work."

"Yeah, great." Who cares about stupid boxes? I'm stuck spending the weekend packing and moving. After my first week of middle school, I'd rather do something fun.

"I saw Trenton's mother at the gym yesterday," Mom says. "She told me she thinks football is extremely dangerous. That's why she doesn't let Trenton play."

"Trenton's no good. That's why he's not out." I throw a couple of sweaters I never wear in the bottom of the box. Starting a new school is enough change. I shouldn't have to move to a new house now, too.

"Jackson," Mom says. "I know this isn't your first choice, but I expect you to make the best of it."

"I haven't even seen where we're moving."

"We're doing that tonight," Mom says. "Ted's making a special dinner and Heather and Haley are helping. They are all going out of their way to be nice. I suggest that you reciprocate."

"What?" I stuff some long-sleeved shirts in the box.

"Reciprocate. Be nice." Mom pulls the shirts out of the box. "Fold these properly. They're good shirts."

I open my dresser and pull out a stack of T-shirts and put them in the box. I set the long-sleeved shirts on the bed and start folding them up. All my friends are out having a good time while I'm forced to pack up to move to a place I don't want to go.

I'm wearing my dress-up clothes to dinner at Ted's house. I've got empty seats on either side of me for Heather and Haley because Ted wants us to sit boy-girl-boy-girl since there are three boys and three girls now. Heather, who's wearing black slacks and a tan sweater, carries a bowl of mashed potatoes, and Haley, who's got on a sparkly purple dress, sets a bread basket in front of Mom.

"That's such a pretty dress," Mom says. "And your barrette matches."

"Thank you." Haley smoothes out her dress.

Ted carves the turkey at a center island in the kitchen, and he insists that Mom, Quinn, and I sit while everything is delivered to the table.

Mom takes a sip of her white wine. "We won't argue with that."

"You've done enough with all that packing." Ted carries the platter that's overflowing with turkey.

"Isn't this nice?" Mom says.

"Yeah," Quinn agrees. "I love turkey."

"We decided to have a Thanksgiving meal a couple of months early," Ted announces. "We all have so much to be thankful for, and Heather and Haley and I are thankful that you are moving in here."

I scrunch up my napkin. I can't stand this. The girls probably hate us moving in. If I was in their place, I would.

"I'm thankful, too, that we've got enough room so that each one of you will have your own bedroom," Ted says. "We know this is a big change, and we think it's important that you have your own space."

Heather places a bowl of squash with melted brown sugar

in front of me and I watch her face, but she doesn't reveal much. Everybody is trying *so* hard to be nice that it's making it worse. If Ted, Heather, and Haley were mean and selfish, it would be easier to dislike them.

Mom's looking over like she wants me to say something, but I can't.

"How do you like your room, Jackson?" Ted forces the issue.

"Fine."

Mom sits up and steps on my toe under the table.

"It's big," I say.

"Excellent." Ted grins.

What am I supposed to say? How I'm really feeling? Mom knows I wish we'd gotten our own place. Ted probably does, too. I've already got a dad. I don't need somebody else pretending to be that.

CHAPTER 15

Sunday morning, I pace around the bedroom that's not mine anymore. All my stuff has been moved out, and the bed, dresser, and bookshelf that remain belong to Liz and Jeff.

"Final check!" Ted calls out as two young guys he hired from the country club carry the last boxes downstairs.

I check the closet where empty plastic hangers look lonely. I walk over to the window and look at the lake below. A few of the trees outside are beginning to change to orange and gold.

"Be careful with those boxes," Mom tells the movers. "I don't want any of my vases broken."

"The truck is packed full!" Quinn races into the room. "Let's go!"

We walk downstairs together.

"That's it." Mom straightens a card next to the bottle of champagne she's left for Liz and Jeff on the table.

"Pretty smooth." Ted beams. "We've got two cars. Who wants to ride with me?"

Quinn takes a step toward Mom and I can tell he doesn't. I don't want to, either.

"Jackson, why don't you go with Ted?" Mom says.

"Off we go," Ted says cheerfully.

"Wait," I say. "I need a last check of my room." I bound up the stairs of the place I've stayed for a year. I get down on my knees to look under the bed and see something red against the wall. It's only one of Quinn's Matchbox cars, but I grab it and put it in my pocket. I take one last look around. So long, room.

Everybody's waiting for me downstairs.

"Here." I hand the Corvette to Quinn.

"Thanks. I've been searching for that."

Ted puts his hand on my shoulder and we walk past the movers arranging the last boxes. "We got the truck that was exactly the right size," he says. "I love it when it works out that way."

I slide into the passenger seat of his car, and Ted turns on the AC even though it's not that hot out. "The movers will do all the unloading on the other end," he says. "All we have to do is the unpacking."

I look out at the lawn and the fading flowers as we drive up the long driveway for the final time.

"How's middle school going?" Ted asks.

"Good." I'm getting sick of everybody asking.

"Heather loves sixth grade at Twin Park," he says. "You always have that option if you want to transfer to someplace closer to our house."

"No. I'm staying where I am."

"Of course you want to be with your friends," Ted says. "Your mom says you're playing football with them. How's that going?"

"Good." I stare out the window hoping he'll get the message that I don't want to talk. I wish he didn't try so hard all the time.

We drive west on Border Parkway. We're going the opposite direction from where Dad lives, where my friends live, and where I go to school. I'm going to be farther away from everything now.

———

*H*eather and Haley have arranged plates of doughnuts on the dining room table when we arrive. Mom must have told Ted that Quinn and I love doughnuts.

"Thanks." I pick up a chocolate one covered with dark sprinkles and take a bite.

"Yum." Quinn picks out one with chocolate frosting.

Heather passes on the doughnuts and gets a blueberry yogurt for herself from the fridge. It must be weird having new people move into her house. Haley sits across from Quinn and they lick frosting off their doughnuts. She seems more like him, able to go along with things.

The movers start hauling boxes in and putting them in rooms based on the labels. I finish my doughnut and go downstairs to my bedroom. Ted's house is huge, bigger than Liz and Jeff's, and way bigger than Dad's. It's a split-level with a three-car garage. All the other bedrooms are upstairs. I'm down here with my own bathroom away from everybody else.

I sit in the corner of the empty room and wait for some of my boxes to be brought down. Half of the room is below-ground and half is above. "Garden level," Ted called it.

In the closets the shelves are all bare. The single bed has a mattress and box spring, but no sheets. I imagined it was going to feel crowded when all of us were here together, but it doesn't.

It feels empty.

Dad comes to pick us up at four, and even though I'm ready to go, Mom invites him in to see our new bedrooms.

"That's a good idea," he says.

Mom introduces Dad to Ted in the living room. They shake hands and Ted grasps Dad's hand with both of his. Ted, who's wearing khaki pants and a peach-colored polo shirt, tells Dad what fine young men he has for sons.

"They're good kids." Dad shoves his hands in the pockets of his jeans.

"Good?" Ted grins. "Jackson and Quinn are outstanding. You have a lot to be proud of."

Dad looks around. He doesn't talk like this and doesn't seem to know what to say.

"Now I have somebody I want you to meet," Ted says as Mom ushers Heather and Haley in.

Dad turns from Ted to watch them.

"These are my exceptional daughters." Ted puts his hands on their shoulders. "Heather is eleven and Haley is seven."

"Nice to meet you," Dad greets them. Everybody stands around and makes small talk.

I break away from the group and wave to Dad. I escort him down to my room, but there's not much to show. It's just a bedroom.

"You've got nice light," Dad says.

I stand waiting.

"How do you like it?" Dad asks.

"It's okay."

"Let's go see Quinn's. Then we'll go to the pool."

"How come G-Man didn't come with you?"

"He's going to meet us there," Dad says. "I thought that might be best."

G-Man doesn't always say the most appropriate things, but I still wish he was here. I'd like to see what he'd say to Ted.

The three of us sit in the hot tub at the Y and wait for G-Man, who's running late. I slip down so the hot water comes up to my chin and listen to the burbling bubbles.

"There he is," Quinn says.

G-Man scurries down the pool deck carrying his towel and goggles. He's wearing his long swim trunks that have green and yellow flowers on them. They look ridiculous, but he says they're in style and we're not keeping up with what's new.

"Hey, boys," he says. "Sorry I'm late. I had a few deals on eBay that I had to close. I picked up some more Obama buttons at a good price." He hangs up his towel on a hook.

G-Man collects unusual things like political buttons, and he likes telling us about them.

"Those buttons will go up in value," he says, "because that was such a historic election." He splashes into the tub. "Why so serious, boys?"

"They're tired," Dad says. "Their mom moved into a new place with them and they've been packing and unpacking."

"We moved into Ted's house," Quinn says.

"Aye, yay, yay," G-Man says.

Dad looks at him sternly.

"I was just saying 'aye, yay, yay.'" G-Man positions himself on his favorite jet. "Last time I checked it's still a free country. A fellow can say 'aye, yay, yay' if he wants."

"Aye, yay, yay," Quinn says.

"That's the way, Quinny." G-Man turns to me. "Did you find out where Señora O'Reilly's people come from?"

"No. I forgot."

"What's the matter with your memory?" He splashes me. "You ask her."

"Okay." I sit up and splash him back.

"How's football?"

"I switched to defense."

"That's smart," G-Man says. "Every knucklehead wants to play offense and score touchdowns. They think that's the way to get a girlfriend."

"What's the way to get a girlfriend?" Quinn asks.

"It's not that complicated, Quinnster." G-Man lounges back to position his shoulder on the jet. "Talk to them. Ask questions. Most people love talking about themselves."

"True." Dad nods.

"Defense is fun," G-Man says. "Where's Diego playing?"

"He hasn't come out yet."

"What's he waiting for?"

"His parents think football's too dangerous."

"Aye, yay, yay," G-Man says. "Life's dangerous. Football's a great game."

"I know. That's what I told him. But somebody needs to talk with his parents and they both speak Spanish. Will you do it, G-Man?"

"What do you want me to say?"

"That Diego promised us he'd come out. That we need him on the team."

"I'll think about it." G-Man shifts his other shoulder onto the jet.

I sink down into the bubbles and wish the water would wash away some of my mixed-up feelings about football, middle school, the move, Mom and Ted, and everything else.

CHAPTER 16

When I get to school Monday morning, there's a yellow sign taped to my locker.

THIS LOCKER
IS DEEMED INOPERABLE!
REPORT TO THE OFFICE IMMEDIATELY!

What does that mean? I take off my sweatshirt, shove it in my backpack, and walk down to the office. On a gray, dreary Monday morning, this is the last thing I need.

In the office Mr. Norquist is lecturing some students about "inappropriate language that is not fitting for Longview Middle School students."

I tell the secretary about the sign on my locker and she asks what number it is.

"I don't remember."

"You don't know your own locker number?" She looks up over the top of her glasses. "What grade are you in?"

"Sixth."

"Uh-huh," she says like this explains everything.

I give her my name and she finds my information on her computer.

"That locker is inoperable," she announces.

"What does that mean? Where am I supposed to put my stuff?"

"I don't know anything about that." She points over her shoulder at a woman with two boys lined up at her desk. "Ms. Christie is the locker lady."

I take a seat and wait. At this rate, I'm going to be late for homeroom.

When my turn finally comes long after the bell has rung, I give her my name, and she checks her screen.

"Your old locker can't be fixed so we've given you a new locker." She prints out a paper and hands it to me.

"What's this?"

"The number of your new locker and the combination." She takes a map from a tray and draws a red X on it. "Here's the location."

"You mean it's not by my old locker?"

"No, all of those are already assigned. The only lockers left are in the seventh-grade section."

"I don't want a locker there."

"Sorry. You don't have a choice."

I can't believe it. Everybody else is in the sixth-grade section and I've got to go off on my own. The red X on the map makes me think of pirates, seventh-grade pirates.

"Here's a late pass." Ms. Christie hands me another slip. "Do you know how to find your new locker?"

"Yeah." I set off with a queasy feeling in my stomach. Why did I have to get a bad locker?

I turn the corner and just about die from a heart attack. Sunglasses and Spike Head, the two eighth graders from the bus, are coming my way.

I duck back behind a locker. What are they doing in the hall after the bell? I sneak back around the corner and go all the way around the long way, listening for any voices and peeking around every corner before I move forward.

When I finally find my new locker, I keep looking around to make sure I'm not being followed. I spin the combination and am surprised when it opens easily. All my stuff is inside. It got moved from my old locker as if by magic.

Even though this locker works better, I wish I was still in the sixth-grade section. I'd rather have my jammed one than be down here on my own.

In the afternoon on my way to Spanish, I stop at the bathroom in the main hall, the same one I used last spring on our school visit. So far I've only used the bathrooms in the sixth-grade section or the gym, but I need one now. I rush in and stop dead in my tracks.

Sunglasses and Spike Head squeeze a sixth grader up against the wall by the paper-towel dispenser.

"Where's your bathroom rent, Sixer?" Sunglasses growls.

"Hand it over or you'll get the swirlie of a lifetime," Spike Head threatens.

I turn around to escape but Spike Head slides over and blocks my way.

"Give me your bathroom rent, Sixer." He leans in and looks me over. "You're the sixer from the bus who eats rabbit food." I smell his mustard breath.

The other kid uncrumples some bills from his pocket.

"Get out of here," Sunglasses says. "Don't say a word to anyone." He turns toward me. "Hand it over."

I reach into my pocket but don't have any money.

"Swirlie time." Spike Head spins me around and pushes me toward a stall.

"Wait." I hold up my hands. "I'll bring it tomorrow."

"Too late." Sunglasses grabs my arm and marches me forward. I knew I shouldn't have come in here. I should have gone all the way down to the sixth-grade section.

"Let him go," a deep voice rumbles.

Sunglasses turns, but he keeps squeezing my arm. It's the gigantic guy from the bus, the one I helped with his phone.

"What's your problem, Tiny?" Spike Head asks.

"Let him go."

Sunglasses drops my arm and I rush forward. I want to say thanks but decide it's best to keep moving.

I turn and race down the hall.

"No running," a hall monitors shouts.

I slow to a speed walk as I try to get as far away from Sunglasses and Spike Head as I possibly can.

In Spanish, I stand in front of Señora O'Reilly's desk before class starts. I hate doing stuff like this, but G-Man will keep bugging me until I give him an answer.

"Señora O'Reilly."

"Sí, Julio."

107

"My grandpa is Irish. I mean his ancestors are Irish. Mine are, too."

"*Sí.*" She tries to figure out why I'm talking about the Irish in Spanish class.

"Anyway my grandpa wants to know where your ancestors came from in Ireland." I try to remember some of the names he said. "He wants to know if you're related to Donovans or Kennedys."

She shakes her head. "O'Reilly is my husband's name. My maiden name is Jaworski. Tell your grandpa I'm one-hundred-percent Polish."

I shuffle back to my seat as kids watch me like I was trying to suck up and failed. G-Man doesn't realize how extreme some of his ideas are.

At football practice, I pick a wet leaf off my cleats. Last week felt like summer, but today the cool, moist air feels like fall. I'm playing left defensive end as we go against our offense, and the linebacker behind me is Speros, aka the Jerk.

"Hut, hut." Isaac takes the snap and pitches to Gig who runs to my side. I stay on the outside shoulder of the guy blocking me, but Gig turns on the speed and tries to beat me to the sideline. I close in on him, but he sticks out a stiff arm against my shoulder pads. I reach for him but slip and fall down. Gig races past and beats everybody downfield for a touchdown.

"Tackle strong, Kennedy," Coach Tanglen shouts. "Don't go in tentatively."

"Turn the play in, Kennedy," Speros says.

Gig loops by me as he runs back. "You should have stayed on offense, Julio."

I line up at end and rub the goose bumps on my arms. I should have worn long sleeves under my jersey.

"Hut." Isaac drops back to pass but hands off to Gig on a draw.

"Draw," we holler out the play. I fight through my blocker and crash down the line. Another blocker charges toward me and I stick my hand out.

Ahhhh. My thumb gets bent back on his helmet. I pull it away and the blocker plows over me as Gig cuts inside for a big gain.

I get up slowly and wrap my right hand around my left thumb. I clench my teeth as I walk back to the huddle. Across the way, G-Man pulls into the parking lot and peers over the steering wheel.

"Hut, hut, hut." Isaac pitches to Gig, who comes my way again. Are they running at me on purpose?

I stay outside, the way I'm supposed to, and Gig ducks in to cut up. Suddenly he bounces back outside and I'm caught flat-footed. Gig races around me again and I dive for the tackle, but get nothing. Gig outraces Speros and Cerrato down the sideline and dances into the end zone.

"Kennedy, don't get beat outside," Coach Tanglen shouts. "I thought you said you knew how to play defensive end."

"Turn it in," Speros screams at me. "Do it right!"

"Defense, you're going to need to play a lot better than that tomorrow against the Hawks," Coach says.

On the other side of the ball, the offensive players are giving each other chest bumps and goofing around. I hold my thumb, which throbs with pain.

Nothing's going right on defense. I should have stayed with Gig and Isaac.

CHAPTER 17

By the end of practice it's started to rain and I'm glad G-Man is already here.

"The defense looks bad," he says. "Usually at the start of the season, the defense is ahead of the offense. You guys aren't getting any pressure up front. You need someone who's strong and quick."

"Yeah." I squeeze my thumb gently as I sit in the passenger seat.

"Call Diego," G-Man says. "See if he's home. Ask if his parents are there."

I press Diego's number and he says his mom is home, but his dad is working. I relay this to G-Man, who says, "Tell him we have something to drop off."

I do this, though I'm not sure what's up.

"What's the matter with your thumb?" G-Man sees me grabbing it.

"Jammed it on a helmet."

"Is that why you were playing so cautiously out there?"

"Yeah," I say, even though I was playing that way before the injury.

G-Man inspects it while we stop at a light. "Does this hurt?" He touches the tip of the thumb.

"No."

"This?" He presses at the base.

"No."

"This?" He touches the knuckle.

"*Yowwwww!*"

"You need to get some ice on that."

We pull into a gas station and G-Man asks for a plastic bag and explains it's an emergency when the clerk doesn't want to give him one without a purchase. She finally does after he says he buys gas here all the time. We go over to the beverage dispenser and G-Man fills up the bag with ice and ties it closed.

"Here. Wrap this around your thumb. That will slow down the swelling."

Back in the car, G-Man quizzes me on how much

Spanish I've learned. I keep reminding him that I've only been in class for a week.

"What's Señora O'Reilly teaching you, Gaelic?"

"She's not Irish at all. Her husband is. She's one-hundred-percent Polish."

"Aye, yay, yay."

My hand starts to get numb from the ice so I set the bag on the floor.

"Keep it on there a little longer," G-Man says. "Ice early makes a big difference."

He doesn't ask for any directions as he turns by Target. G-Man is like that. If he's been someplace once, he remembers how to get there.

"We need to work on a couple of phrases so you're ready." He says something in Spanish and has me repeat it over and over trying to improve my pronunciation. "Leave the ice here and don't hold your thumb when we're in there. We don't want Señora Jimenez seeing any football injuries."

At Diego's apartment building, G-Man takes a chocolate-raspberry cake out from the trunk.

"That's a huge cake."

"You don't go visiting someone without bringing something." He hands me the cake. "Don't they teach you anything in school these days?"

I carry the cake as G-Man holds the door to the entryway. He finds JIMENEZ on the directory and buzzes the number.

"Yeah," Diego answers.

"I'm here with G-Man," I say into the speaker.

"Come on up. Apartment 206." He buzzes us in.

G-Man and I climb the stairs and walk down a hallway that has bright green carpet with orange suns on it. It's a candidate for the ugliest carpeting in the history of floor coverings.

Diego opens the door of 206.

"Hey," I say.

He looks at me like I'll give him an explanation, but I just stand there holding the cake.

His mother, who's working in the kitchen, wipes her hands on a dish towel. G-Man gives me a poke in the back.

"*Hola, Señora Jimenez.*"

"*Hola.*" She seems surprised.

"*Traemos un pastel.*" I say the words G-Man taught me about bringing the cake.

"*Gracias.*" She smiles.

G-Man starts talking a mile a minute in Spanish as we sit down at the kitchen table. The apartment is small, and the walls are covered with family photographs, including one of Angela, Diego's cousin who was with us at soccer camp last month. I look at that one longer than any of the others.

Señora Jimenez says something to Diego, and he gets up and sets out plates and forks for each of us. She slices big pieces of cake and goes to the stove and returns with a pot that smells good.

"*Chocolate caliente,*" she says and even I can tell what that is.

She pours four cups of hot chocolate as G-Man talks away in Spanish. Occasionally I catch a word I recognize like *Gig, Isaac,* or *football,* but I don't know what he's telling her. Diego swings his head from G-Man to his mom like he's watching a tennis match.

I blow on the hot chocolate and take a sip. It's good. Not as sweet as usual but more thick and chocolaty. I keep my injured thumb beneath the table. I thought the ice was supposed to help, but it's still raging with pain.

After everybody is finished, G-Man stands and I follow. He gives me a nudge and I remember our practice in the car. "*Mil gracias.*"

"*De nada*," Señora Jimenez says. "*Mil gracias*."

Diego walks us to the door.

"Thanks," he says.

"*De nada*," I reply. Even I'm picking up a few things.

"**S**eñora Jimenez is going to talk with her husband," G-Man says in the car. "She's still worried about football, but she recognizes how important you, Gig, and Isaac are to Diego and how much fun you had together playing baseball and soccer."

"Soccer camp wasn't *that* fun." I hold the bag of ice on my thumb.

"It was fun for Diego to have you there. How's your thumb feeling?"

"Bad." I hold it up and it's already swollen and turning purple.

"We better stop at the clinic and have them take an X-ray. Call your dad and tell him we'll be late."

I dial Dad and give him the news.

"I don't think it's broken," G-Man says, "but we'll get it checked out."

I wrap the bag of ice around my hand. I've jammed fingers before, but the thumb feels way worse.

CHAPTER 18

At Urgent Care, a lot of people are already waiting. The guy across from me has a blood-soaked cloth wrapped around his right hand and he's holding it above his head to slow down the bleeding. A mom sits next to a little girl who's gasping for air from an asthma attack. G-Man tells the girl to concentrate on blowing the air out and that she's going to be okay and she smiles weakly.

We wait and wait and wait. G-Man reads two newspapers and a *Newsweek* while I page through old issues of *Sports Illustrated*.

"Jackson Kennedy," a nurse finally calls.

G-Man and I follow her into a small examining room that has a super-clean medical-clinic smell.

"How'd you hurt your thumb?" She checks her clipboard.

"Football."

"That figures," she says. "Are you left-handed?"

"No."

"It could be worse. It could be your right hand."

She asks a few more questions and says the doctor will be in shortly. But he's not.

"It could be worse," G-Man says. "You could have broken your neck."

"Yeah, it could be worse. I could be dead."

We wait forever before the doctor finally comes in, and he looks at my thumb for two seconds and says we need to go upstairs for an X-ray.

"We could have gone there right away," G-Man says as we wait for the elevator. "We knew they'd need a picture."

At X-ray we wait a long time before the technician calls us in and has me wear a heavy apron around my waist.

"What's this for?"

"To protect you from the radiation," she says.

"To protect your private parts," G-Man adds.

The technician has me hold my hand in three different positions while a big camera with hoses attached snaps pictures. "We'll send these right down to Urgent Care," she says.

Back at Urgent Care we wait and wait some more before the doctor finally comes in.

"Good news." He pulls up the X-rays on his screen. "Your thumb isn't broken, but you have a pretty bad sprain. We'll fix you up with a splint and a bandage to wrap around it. Make an appointment for three weeks with your doctor to see how it's healing. Until then, resume your normal activities."

"What about football?" I ask.

The doctor pushes his glasses up. "I'm not going to prohibit it, but the best approach would be to forget about football for this year."

G-Man rubs his forehead. I was afraid the doctor would say that. I finally get Diego to come out and now I'm done.

"Thanks, Doc." G-Man shakes his hand.

Yeah, thanks. The doctor doesn't look like he ever played football in his life or knows how huge it is to miss a whole season.

When the nurse comes back in, she fits a metal-and-foam splint to my thumb that goes all the way up my wrist and wraps it with elastic tape that sticks to itself.

"Keep this splint on," she says. "It's a good idea when you get home to elevate your hand as much as possible and to ice it to slow the swelling." She hands me an Instant Cold Pack.

"Only take this bandage and tape off when you ice it.

Otherwise keep it on for protection." She wraps the bandage tighter and tighter around my thumb and wrist as I feel football slipping away.

Out in the hall, G-Man stops me. "Why the long face?"

"I can't miss the season."

"Who says you have to? You heard the doctor. He didn't prohibit it. You have a sprain and there are ways to protect that." G-Man holds up his pinkie finger. "I played with a cast senior year of high school."

"But he said I should forget about football for this season."

"Do you think not playing would make you forget about it?"

"No."

"He said to resume your normal activities. Is football part of your normal activities?"

"Yeah."

"You love playing?

"Yeah."

"That's what I thought." G-Man puts his hand on my shoulder. "I'll talk to your dad. You take care of it with your mom."

———

Quinn is curious about my wrapped hand. "You look like a mummy."

"Does it hurt?" Dad gets me a plate of pork chops and potatoes since they already ate.

"No, not bad."

I scoop up potatoes while Dad discusses the doctor visit with G-Man. I'm starving after getting back so late. Dad sees me struggling to cut the pork chop, and he reaches over and cuts up my food like he used to when I was little kid.

After I finish, I retreat to my bedroom to call Mom. "Hi, how are things going?"

"What's wrong?" It's like she has mind-reading powers.

"Nothing." I pick at a piece of pork caught between my teeth.

"Jackson, what's wrong?"

I pause. "I've got some good news and some bad news. Which do you want first?"

"What happened? What's the bad news?"

"I got hurt today."

"How?"

"I sprained my left thumb on a helmet at practice, but G-Man took me to the doctor and we got it all fixed up." I try to sound as upbeat as possible.

"Oh, Jackson, I was worried something like this was going to happen. I told you football is dangerous."

"Mom, you were worried about a concussion. That's the good news. My brain's fine. No concussion."

The hardest part of having a splint is keeping it dry all the time. I can't even wash my hands the regular way so I have to wipe my fingers that stick out of the bandage with a washcloth. When I take a shower, I have to wrap my hand in a plastic Target bag, slip a rubber band around it, and hold it over my head. I have to squeeze shampoo directly onto my hair and rub it in with one hand while I hold the other up like I'm waiting to be called on by a teacher. Everything takes longer with my hand wrapped up, even something as simple as buttoning my shirt.

At the bus stop on Tuesday, Isaac's mouth drops open. "What happened?"

"Sprained thumb."

"Are you done?"

"No. G-Man's getting me a pad to protect it."

"Good. We need you."

When I get to school I'm worried about going into the seventh-grade section for my locker, but nobody bothers me. The two girls whose lockers I'm in between even talk to me.

"What happened?" the tall girl asks.

"I hurt it in football."

They both crowd closer and ask questions.

"Can we sign it?" the shorter one asks.

"It's not a cast." My locker pops open easily.

"That's okay. We'll sign the bandage."

"I've got a Sharpie." The tall girl writes *Cassie* and dots the *i* with a heart.

"I'm Amanda." The shorter girl prints her name and draws a smiley face next to it.

"I'm Jackson." I pull books out of my backpack. Maybe having a bad thumb isn't the worst thing in the world.

In homeroom, Sydney's concerned and wants to know the whole story. She's never had a splint and wants to know how it feels. She also wants to make sure that Gig didn't do anything to cause it.

"No, it wasn't his fault," I say. "It's just the breaks—or the sprains."

She laughs at my lame joke and wants to sign her name. Who knew girls would be so interested?

Ms. Constantine has me tell the story to the group and even some of the eighth graders who usually ignore sixth graders ask questions.

"Can you still play football?" a boy from the back table asks.

"Yeah," I say, like it's no big deal.

Diego is shocked when I meet him at his locker before gym. "What happened?"

"I sprained it at practice yesterday."

"Before you came to see us?" He looks at my hand and frowns.

"Yeah."

He slams his locker shut. "You had a sprained thumb while your grandpa was telling my mom that I'd be fine if I came out?"

"Yeah, you will be." Cassie and Amanda walk by and I raise my wrapped-up hand to wave.

"Don't let my parents know anything about it or they'll change their minds," Diego says.

"Did they say you could come out?"

"Yeah, my dad signed the slip after talking with my mom."

"Fantastic." I give him a fist bump with my good hand.

"But I'm not playing if you're not."

"Who said I wasn't playing?"

*F*or READ Club, I sit at a table in the library with Sam, Trenton, and Quincy. We eat our bag lunches while we listen to Mr. Amodt. "We'll meet twice a month over lunch period and advisory. I'll have books set out for you and you can take any others you want off the shelves. As READ Club members, you are entitled to check out as many books and magazines as you want."

I bite into my roast beef sandwich. I'm only here because I wanted to go outside last week in advisory.

"Look around the room," Mr. Amodt says.

I see the usual smart kids who like to read. Nothing strange about that since it's called READ Club. Read Every Awesome Day. Yeah, right.

"What do you notice about who is here?" Mr. Amodt asks.

"That we are all eating bag lunches," Trenton offers.

"Yes, very observant," Mr. Amodt says. "What else?"

"That there are more girls than boys," Cassie, my new locker neighbor, says.

"Yes, over two-thirds," Mr. Amodt says. "Why is that?"

"Because girls are better readers," Amanda says.

"Because reading is quiet and boys like to make noise," Sydney offers.

"Because girls are smarter," Kelsey says and other girls laugh.

"What about you boys?" Mr. Amodt says. "Why aren't more boys here?"

"A lot of boys think reading is boring," Sam says.

I raise my hand. "There aren't enough books about things we're interested in."

"Like what?" Mr. Amodt asks.

"Like sports or adventure."

"I've got tons of books on those subjects," Mr. Amodt says. "After you've eaten, you can browse the tables. I've split them up by interest. This table is all sports." He points to a mountain of books. "This one is all historical fiction." He walks over to another one. "This is all adventure. Whatever you're interested in, we'll find books for you."

I eat my last potato chip and shake the crumbs from the bag into my palm and lick them off.

Mr. Amodt walks back up to the front of the room. "Here's your homework. For next READ Club, each one of you has an assignment. Bring a boy with you. No excuses." He pauses. "I'll have some candy. I'm not above a bit of bribery."

Chapter 19

When it's time to look at books, Mr. Amodt notices my mummy hand. "What happened here?"

"Sprained thumb." I pick through books on the sports table with one hand. "I jammed it on a helmet."

"I've seen plenty of those," Mr. Amodt says. "Are you still able to play?"

"Yeah."

"Wrap it up well. What position do you play?"

"Defensive end."

"You should be okay there. Good thing you're not a quarterback."

I pick up a book called *The Boy Who Saved Baseball*, which has a picture of a boy tossing a ball into the air against an orange sky.

"I read that," Sam says. "It's awesome."

I turn it over and see the author has written other books about baseball.

"That's the book I suggested to you." Mr. Amodt watches me.

"When?"

"On your school visit last spring. I remember you got separated from your class and showed up all wide-eyed in the library."

I'd just as soon forget about that.

"There's also a prequel to that book." Mr. Amodt sorts through the books on the table. "Here it is." He hands me a book called *The Desperado Who Stole Baseball* with a baseball, a couple of wooden bats, and a mysterious man on the cover. "You can read them in either order, but I'd like you to check them out and let me know what you think."

"Okay." I've got my books now.

At the desk, Sydney's checking out a pile of books. How's she going to read that much in two weeks? I'm going to have a hard time finishing two.

"Are you really going to play with your splint?" she asks.

"Yeah." I hold it up. "It's no big deal." Having the splint makes me feel tougher. I remember when Noah broke his ankle playing baseball last spring and acted like getting a cast was an accomplishment, some kind of badge of honor. Now I know what he was feeling. When you're injured, people treat you differently, like you did something important.

Because Dad is taking Quinn to his dentist appointment, G-Man drives me to our first game. He told Dad he talked to a friend of his who's a doctor and that the pad he got at the sports store and taped around my hand was fine to protect it.

"Have you told your mom that you're playing with it?" he asks.

"Not yet."

"You need to do that."

"I know." I check the text on my phone. "Diego's at home and says he needs some help getting his equipment on."

"We can't let his mother see you with your hand wrapped up like this," G-Man says. "Tell him to do the best he can and be waiting for us outside. We'll stop on the way and get him fixed up."

I text him back with one hand. I still can't believe he's coming. Isaac and Gig had me convinced he wasn't going to play.

When we pull up, Diego's at the door and he looks like a

football player who's been hit by a tornado. Pads are flapping about, a number's peeling off his jersey, and something about his shoulder pads looks seriously wrong.

"Ready for some football?" G-Man asks him.

"I don't know." Diego climbs in the backseat and looks at my hand. "You can play like that?"

"Yeah." I check out his shoulder pads. "I don't think those are on right."

"Never mind," G-Man says. "We'll stop in the Target parking lot."

When we do, G-Man helps Diego shove the kneepads in properly and figures out that his shoulder pads are on backward. "Who helped you with these?"

"My brother. He's in high school."

"He doesn't know anything about football, does he?"

"No."

"You tie these in front so you can do it yourself next time." G-Man demonstrates.

"We're supposed to tape our names on our helmet," I say.

"Target will have that." G-Man leads us in and Diego and I follow in our pads, up and down the aisles, searching for tape and a Sharpie.

After we buy them, G-Man rips off a piece and gives Diego the Sharpie to write JIMENEZ in bold black letters.

"You're set," G-Man says.

Diego looks over at me. He doesn't look like he feels set at all.

When we get to the field at Echo Park, Diego and I sit down to put our cleats on and I ask G-Man to tie mine since I can't use my padded-up left hand. Diego's wearing his soccer cleats. They're not the same as football cleats, but they'll work.

The Hawks players in their silver jerseys are getting out of SUVs and minivans and I feel a moment of panic. I've been concentrating on getting Diego here and acting cool about my injury, but now I wonder if I am going to be able to play. Across the way, Gig and Isaac are throwing a football. I wait until Diego's got his shoes tied and we walk over together.

"Look who I've got," I holler.

"Diego!" Isaac shouts and gives him a fist bump.

Gig stares at him like he can't believe it. "I didn't think you'd come out, Padre."

"I'm here," Diego says.

"Your hand." Isaac turns to me. "Wrapped up like a present."

Coach Tanglen comes over.

"We've got a new player," Isaac says. "Diego Jimenez. He's going to be good."

"Welcome." Coach shakes Diego's hand and sees me. "What happened to you?"

"Just a sprain. Three weeks in a splint. They said it was okay to play like this." I hold it up.

"If you feel any pain or discomfort, tell me right away," Coach says. "We don't want you doing any damage."

Diego's eyes widen. He's probably wondering what kind of sport this is that you play with a wrapped-up hand.

"What position do you play, Diego?" Coach asks.

"Defensive tackle," I say.

"No, he plays on offense," Isaac says.

"Yeah, Padre's an offensive tackle." Gig pushes forward.

Coach frowns. "I believe I was asking Diego."

"Wherever you want me to play," Diego says. "I haven't played much football."

"He'd be a great tight end," Isaac says.

"No, Ike. Padre would be a better tackle."

Coach holds up his hands. "Last time I checked, you two weren't coaches. We need help on defense and that's going to be easier for Diego since he's a week behind everyone else. Diego, watch Hauser at the position next to Kennedy, defensive tackle. Pay attention to what he does and try to get a feel for the game."

Diego snaps and unsnaps the chinstrap on his helmet and looks more nervous than I've ever seen him before.

CHAPTER 20

I stand next to Diego on the sideline as we start out on offense.

"Hut, hut," Isaac calls. He takes the snap and pitches to Gig. Defenders gang-tackle him at the line of scrimmage.

"Stay with your blocks," Coach Martineau calls out.

I touch the padding around my thumb. It doesn't hurt, but I'm not going to be able to use that hand to push off and protect myself from blockers the way I'm used to. I'm going to have to play with one good hand.

On the next play Isaac hands off to Gig, who plows ahead for a couple of yards.

"Watch their defensive tackle, the second one in from the end of the line," I tell Diego.

"He's running into the guy opposite him and trying to tackle the guy with the ball."

"You've got it. That's defense."

On third and nine, Isaac drops back to throw, but he can't find anybody open. Two Hawks defensive linemen shed their blocks and close in on him. Isaac pulls the ball down and is tackled for a loss.

"Hold your blocks," Coach says.

"Get rid of the ball, Ike." Gig chases after Isaac as they run off the field.

"Nobody was open."

"I was." Gig takes his mouth guard out and spits.

"You always think you're open."

"I usually am." Gig won't let it go.

"Wilkins, use your safety valve when everybody else is covered," Coach says. "Who's your safety valve?"

"Gig," Isaac says quietly.

Sam boots a decent punt, but the Hawks return man runs it back all the way to our forty-yard line. They're starting with good field position.

I snap my chinstrap, tuck in my mouth guard, and run onto the field. I'm glad I play on the left side where my injured hand is away from the ball.

"Down, set, hut," their quarterback calls. On the snap I fend off their end with my arm and bounce off. A sweep comes my way, so I stay outside to string out the play. Help comes from the inside, and Speros and I tackle the running back after a gain of two.

"Good play, Kennedy and Speros," Coach Tanglen calls.

I line up at my spot and enjoy hearing my name called. I can do this. I can play with one hand wrapped up.

On the next play the quarterback drops back to pass, but at the last second hands off to the tailback.

"Draw," we shout. The runner starts forward, stops, and cuts my way. I dive into his legs with my shoulder.

"Good tackle," G-Man hollers out.

"Way to go." Noah slaps me on the back.

I take my place at end. I can't imagine not being out here.

On the next play the quarterback drops back and the running back sneaks out of the backfield. I run over to cover him as the quarterback throws and I reach up for the interception. Instead the ball hits my mummy hand and falls to the ground. I grab the pad on my hand. That hurt. I've got to remember not to stick that hand up when I'm trying to catch.

I should have tipped it with my good hand and tried to cradle it against my chest with my arms. It's a good thing

I'm not on offense as a wide receiver. With this paw, I wouldn't get to play at all.

In the third quarter, the game is still tied zero to zero. I guess G-Man is right that offenses usually struggle more than defenses at the start of the season. We can't get anything going. The Hawks smother everything at the line of scrimmage, and when Isaac drops back to throw, he gets heavy pressure. Even when he does get time, our receivers aren't open or drop the ball.

"How come we can't score?" Diego asks.

"I don't know. Maybe the defense will have to score."

"How?"

"An interception or fumble recovery." I flash back to that interception I could have grabbed in the first quarter. That would have helped.

On third down, Isaac drops back to pass. A Hawks linebacker blitzes from the side and Gig tries to block him low. The linebacker jumps over the block and slashes his arm down to knock the ball out of Isaac's hand.

The ball rolls around and a Hawks defender picks it up and sprints into the end zone. Six to nothing.

"You've got to pick up the blitz, Milroy," Coach Martineau says to Gig as the offense comes off the field.

Isaac glares at Gig. He didn't have a chance. He didn't see the linebacker coming from his blind side.

The Hawks fail on the extra point so it stays six to nothing.

The offense goes back out, but they're arguing about assignments and only gain two yards on three plays and have to punt.

In the fourth quarter, with time running down, Noah twists his ankle when their center rolls over on it. He slowly gets up and hops off to the sideline.

I look over to Coach Tanglen for a substitute. We don't have any extra defensive linemen as subs, so I don't know who he'll send in. Suddenly Diego's running onto the field. I can't believe it. He only showed up today and Coach is letting him play.

I position him next to me. "Wait for the snap count, go as hard as you can, and try to grab the guy with the ball. We need to get the ball back."

Diego nods and puts his mouth guard in.

"Down, set, hut." They run right at Diego. He stands up

his blocker and pushes him back into the tailback who we tackle together for a one-yard loss.

"Great play." I slap his shoulder pads.

"Way to go, Jimenez," Coach Tanglen shouts. "Keep it up."

On the next play, they run a sweep the other way and gain seven yards.

"We've got to hold them here," I shout.

Their quarterback comes to the line and licks his fingers. This is the crucial play of the game. If we stop them here, we still have a chance to score. If they get a first down, they'll run out the clock.

"Down, set." The quarterback pauses. "Hut."

The offensive players all hold their positions, but Diego jumps across and bumps into the tackle. Penalty flags go flying.

"Offsides, red," the referee announces. "Five-yard penalty. First down." He extends his arm and the Hawks jump up and down like they've won the Super Bowl.

"They were going on the second hut," I tell Diego. "The quarterback used a hard count to draw us off."

"To draw me off," Diego says. "I cost us the game."

"No, you didn't." I wipe the dirt and sweat from my face with my sleeve. "The offense has got to score points." I line up at my position on the end. I hope the coaches don't see the problems on offense and decide to move Diego there. We need him on defense. I need him next to me.

CHAPTER 21

I sit down at lunch with Diego and Isaac on Wednesday. "Where's Gig?"

"I haven't seen him," Diego says.

"Me neither." Isaac unwraps his chicken sandwich. "Did you talk with him after the game?"

"Yeah, he was mad we lost." I open my milk carton and take a gulp.

"We all were," Isaac says. "What else did he say?"

"That we have to play better." I'm not going to tell Isaac that Gig complained about not getting the ball enough.

"Here he comes." Diego squeezes mustard on his hot dog.

Gig sits down beside me and bites into his stuffed-crust pizza.

"Where were you?" I ask.

"Ms. Monihan wanted to talk about that group."

"What about it?" I hold out my Hot Cheetos, which I can't manage with one hand. Gig rips the bag open for me.

"She's decided to have two groups. So many kids have family members in the military that she's got enough for two. Sydney and I don't have to be in the same group."

"That's good, right?" I give him a couple of Hot Cheetos.

"Yeah, but kids kept talking. I told Ms. Monihan I hate being late for lunch."

"Hey, how's that READ Club?" Isaac peels a piece of string cheese.

"Okay. Why?"

"Kelsey invited me and I said yes. She was excited to finish her homework."

"I was going to ask you. We each have to recruit a boy for the next meeting." I bite into my pizza burger. "Diego, will you come so I get credit?"

"Sydney already asked me."

I try to think who else I could ask.

"What about me?" Gig rubs cheese off his chin. "Why didn't you ask me?"

"Because you don't like to read."

"Who says? I read stuff in reading lab."

"Will you come to READ Club?"

"No way."

"Why not?"

"Because Squid Face is there."

"Lots of people are. You wouldn't have to sit near Sydney."

"No, but I'm sure she talks all the time."

"She doesn't. And Mr. Amodt is in charge. He's also the seventh-grade football coach. He might be good to know if you want to start next year."

"I'll think about it, Julio."

"Remember your stuff for Friday," Isaac says.

"What's Friday?" Diego finishes off his brownie.

"Spirit Day."

I forgot about it, too. How could I possibly forget about the day eighth graders rule the school?

School has settled into a pattern now. It feels like regular school but with more homework than we got last year. After a full day of classes, I'm glad to end my afternoon with FACS. It's my only class with Isaac, and Mrs. Randall is fun. Best of all, when we have food labs, we get to eat what we make.

"Y'all ready?" Mrs. Randall says. "Split up into your lab groups."

I stand next to Ruby as Bossy Boots reads out our tasks for making cheese bread. Because of my sprained thumb, everybody lets me have the two easiest ones: turning on the oven to three hundred fifty degrees and layering slices of cheese on top of the bread.

"How's football?" Ruby asks.

"We lost yesterday, but we have another game next Tuesday."

"How's playing with a splint?" She looks at my mummy hand.

"Okay. I wrap it up for games and practices. I'm getting so used to it, I even forget about it sometimes."

"I'm doing something after school, too," she says. "I've got a small part in a one-act play. The drama teacher wants us to have the experience of rehearsing and being onstage before we begin work on the fall play, which is going to be *The Music Man*."

"Really, what's your part?"

"I'm Gwendolyn Hartness. I live on a farm and I'm the youngest sister who's kind of spoiled. It requires lots of acting because I'm not like that at all." She sticks her nose in the air and sniffs.

I laugh. "When's the performance?"

"A week from Friday. I've got to memorize my part quickly. We're going so fast so we don't have time to get nervous. Here's a deal," she says. "I'll come to one of your games if you come to our play."

"Okay."

"Deal." She reaches out to shake my hand in a dramatic gesture. Just like a real actress.

At practice, guys are still arguing about the loss before we've even taken the field.

"The offense didn't do anything," Tony says.

"The defense wasn't that great either," Gig shoots back.

"We didn't give up any points," I say. "You can't do better than that."

Coach Martineau walks over and cuts us off. "Nobody played particularly well," he says. "You all have a lot of room for improvement. Put on your helmets and take four laps around the field."

"Four laps?" Gig questions.

"Get going," Coach says. "Any more arguing and I'll make it five. Go!"

I pull down my helmet and snap my chinstrap. Coach Martineau never has us start practice by running with our helmets on. It feels like a punishment, which isn't fair. The defense didn't give up any points. We shouldn't be blamed for the offense being so bad.

When we break up for our drills, Diego shadows me on defense. He's fast and strong and picks things up quickly. You'd never know this game was new for him.

"Good intensity, Jimenez," Coach Tanglen says. "You can be a force out there."

Noah is hobbling around on his sprained ankle on the sideline. He's not going to be back in the lineup anytime soon.

"Let's practice some stunts," Coach says. "We need to get more pressure on the quarterback." He demonstrates how he wants us to loop around on the end in a passing situation.

"Jimenez, you'll push to the left and run into Kennedy's blocker. Kennedy, you'll loop inside, and while Jimenez is occupying your man, you'll have a wide-open shot at the quarterback." Coach calls out signals and has us practice the timing. Diego cuts to the left and I curl inside.

"Kennedy, you've got to make contact with your blocker so he doesn't know what's happening right away. You've got to make him think he blocked you." Coach demonstrates by banging into me and sliding away.

We practice it over and over, and I'm ready to try it in a game. I want Diego to take care of two linemen so I've got a free shot at the quarterback.

CHAPTER 22

When Mom picks me up after practice on Thursday, she's shocked that I'm in my uniform. "I can't believe you're playing football. I thought you were helping the coaches or getting the players water or something like that."

"I'm not a water boy. I'm a starter." I slide in the front seat. "The doctor and coaches say I can play."

"I don't like this one bit." Mom focuses on my hand. "I need to talk with your father. You should not be playing football with a splint on."

"It's only a sprain, and I wrap it up to protect it."

"I don't care. This isn't even something we should have to discuss."

I buckle my seat belt. "Where's Quinn?"

"Ted took him to Target to get a couple of new cars."

I tilt my seat back and stare out the window. I don't want Mom talking to Dad about this. I don't want her stopping me from playing after I finally got Diego out and we're playing together.

"Do you have homework tonight?" Mom pushes up her sunglasses.

"Yeah." I actually got most of it done in advisory, but I want to keep it as an excuse in case something is planned that I don't want to do.

When we get to Ted's house, Mom presses the garage-door opener. Ted's car isn't here so he and Quinn must still be shopping.

Inside, it feels like we're breaking into someone else's house. Even with our stuff here, it doesn't feel like home.

"I'm going to do homework." What I really mean is I'm going to my room where I can be by myself. Homework is an excuse adults don't usually question.

"We'll continue this discussion later," Mom warns.

For dinner, Mom's made steak, baked potatoes, and green beans, and she's arranged the table so Ted sits next to Quinn and directly across from me. That's the way we used to sit with Dad at the old house. Ted and Quinn talk excitedly about dump trucks and race cars while I watch Mom and try to figure out if she's talked to Dad.

"I heard about your injury," Ted says. "Good thing it's your left hand."

"Yeah." I remember my joke with G-Man. Good thing I'm not dead.

"This steak is great," Quinn says.

"How's Ms. Q.?" I get Quinn talking, and he goes into detail about how Connor threw up right in the middle of story time and it sprayed on the rug. Mom holds up her hands.

"Not now. That's not an appropriate dinnertime topic. Besides we have something serious to discuss." She turns to me. "Playing football while wearing a splint is not a good idea. I haven't talked to your father yet, but I expect him to agree that you need to stop."

I pick at my potato. I didn't expect her to react so severely. I guess I should have told her right away.

"What did your dad say?" Ted wipes his mouth with his napkin.

"What?"

"What did he say about you playing with the splint?"

"He said it was okay as long as I wrapped it up and

protected it." I push green beans around on my plate. "And he said I should call Mom and talk to her about it."

"And did you do that?" Mom raises her voice.

"No."

"Why not?"

"Because I was afraid you'd react this way and make me quit. I wanted to practice with it for a couple of days to prove it was okay."

"Has it been okay?" Ted asks.

"Yeah, it's been fine."

"What are you saying, Ted?" Mom looks at him intently.

"Heather's best friend, Erin, broke her thumb last year playing soccer, but she wanted desperately to finish the season. Her doctor said it was okay to play with a cast. We went to her championship game and she scored the winning goal."

"Football's different from soccer," Mom says sharply.

"I know." Ted holds out his hands to calm things down. "But if it's okay with Jackson's doctor and coaches, maybe it's all right for him to keep playing. I know how important sports and his friends are to him."

I look across at Ted. I can't believe he's sticking up for me like this.

Mom turns to me and seems surprised. "I still don't like it."

"I know."

"Make sure you wrap that hand properly. If you reinjure that thumb I'm going to kill you."

"Then I'd really be injured." I take a bite of steak, and Ted laughs. Who would have ever thought he'd come through like this?

The next morning, I'm dressed for Spirit Day. I've got on white sweatpants, white socks, white shoes, and a red long-sleeved T-shirt. Eighth graders can make you do anything they want if they catch you not wearing white and red.

At the bus stop, Isaac's wearing red pants and a white shirt.

"Did you buy those pants for Spirit Day?" I ask.

"No, I found them in the back of my closet."

"I wouldn't go telling people that." He's the only friend I've got who owns a pair of red pants.

"Are you wearing all white and red?" he asks.

"Everything, including my underwear."

"Me, too. Gig said if you don't have white and red on, the eighth graders make you take your pants off to see if your underwear is white or red. If that's not, they make you take that off, too."

I'm glad I'm prepared. Back by the wall, Tiny, the huge guy who saved me in the bathroom, listens to his iPod. He's wearing his Longview game jersey. I knew he had to be on the eighth-grade football team. I nod, but he's lost in his music.

When the bus comes, we take our usual seats in the middle. Everybody is wearing white and red. The message got out.

At the next stop, Trenton gets on and he's wearing a white sweatshirt and blue jeans.

"Where's your red, Sixer?" Sunglasses calls from the back.

Isaac whips off his belt and hands it to Trenton.

"Here it is." Trenton holds up the red belt.

"We want more red next time," Spike Head warns.

"Why don't you have any red on?" I hit Trenton on the arm.

"I thought it was white *or* red,"

"White *and* red," Isaac says. "Put that belt on so you've got both."

"You saved me." Trenton loops it around his waist.

At school, the halls are filled with red and white. Students are wearing every imaginable combination. Teachers are decked out, too, including Señora O'Reilly, who's wearing a white dress and a red sombrero. Even Assistant Principal Norquist has gotten into it with a red shirt and a white tie with red polka dots. He looks exactly like a circus clown.

The eighth graders roam around and if they find a sixer who's not wearing white and red they draw a big *L* on his face with red marker and give him a warning. But the stories about the eighth graders making students strip down and do anything they want are exaggerated.

They're just designed to terrify us.

I pass the Wall of Heroes and stop to examine a new addition.

ROB MILROY

DAD OF GIG MILROY (AND SYDNEY)

ARMY NATIONAL GUARD

CURRENTLY SERVING IN AFGHANISTAN

In the picture, Gig and his dad are standing side by side in front of the fence in their backyard. They both have their baseball hats on backward and are grinning and giving thumbs-up.

At the game on Tuesday, I'm surprised to see Ted, Mom, and Quinn in the bleachers. Maybe Mom's here to make sure I don't get hurt. G-Man's across the way walking along the sideline. He likes being close to the action and following the plays. He also doesn't like sitting down at games.

I check the bleachers again, but the person I'm looking for isn't here.

"We're going to need a strong game against the Rams," Coach Martineau says. "We're going to put some points on the board."

I crowd in close behind Isaac. It's a warm September day, great for football.

"Play hard," Coach says. "Give it everything you've got when you're on the field."

"Get psyched, Julio." Gig pounds me on my shoulder pads and I pound him back one-handed. Diego walks by and I do the same to him and he looks at me like I'm crazy. Isaac takes a football out of the ball bag and tosses it to Gig, who catches it and throws to me. I tip it with my good hand but drop the catch.

"Let's go, Red Storm." A clear voice sings out. I turn and she's here. Ruby is sitting in the bleachers with a friend.

I forgot to tell her I'm number 83. I want to wave so she knows who I am, but I guess it's obvious. I'm the only one with a mummy hand.

I spread my arms so it's easy for her to see and wait for the whistle for the kickoff. Sam gets off a deep kick and we fly downfield. I slide around the first Ram blocker and crash into a second as the return man cuts outside. Diego lowers his shoulder and brings him down with a hard tackle.

"Way to go." I offer him a hand and pull him up.

"This is fun," he says.

"I told you you'd like football." I glance over in Ruby's direction as I take my spot on the end of the line.

"Hut, hut." On the first play the Rams throw a quick out and Tony Cerrato misses the tackle. The receiver cuts inside and beats everybody to the end zone. Six to nothing. We hardly had time to get set and we're behind.

"Come on, defense," Gig calls out.

The Rams run a quick pitch to the other side for the two-point conversion. I'm embarrassed as we jog to the sideline. We were out there for two plays and gave up eight points. The way our offense has been playing that's a big hole.

Dante makes a nice return to give us the ball at our thirty-three. On the first play, Isaac pitches to Gig and he darts and weaves for a gain of twenty-one.

"Way to go, Gig," Diego yells.

Isaac fires a slant to Quincy who stretches for another first down. The offense is sharper today. Whatever they've been doing in practice is paying off.

On first and ten from their twenty, Isaac drops back and everybody's covered. A Rams defender closes in on him, but Isaac ducks and the defender goes flying past. Isaac turns and passes to Gig who races for the sideline. He's got one guy to beat. Gig fakes inside and the defender lunges. Gig cuts back the other way and dances into the end zone.

We all go wild and I hold my good hand up for Diego to slap. Our first score of the year.

"That's the way," Coach Martineau shouts.

The game goes back and forth. Our offense is making plays and scoring points, but so is theirs. They're using a lot of quick passes and their speedy receivers are burning our defensive backs. We could use somebody fast like Gig or Dante back there, but we need them on offense.

Diego and I are getting good pressure up front, but the Rams aren't running our way. They've got two big guys on the left side of their line and when they're not throwing quick passes for big gains, they're running behind them.

With a couple of minutes left in the game, we're down by seven and Coach Tanglen calls the stunt Diego and I practiced this week. On the snap, Diego pushes left and his blocker sticks with him. I shoulder into my man and bounce back while Diego plows into my guy. I loop around and have a wide-open shot at the quarterback. He's looking to the side to pass, and I lower my shoulder and smash into him and the ball pops lose.

"Fumble!" everybody hollers.

There's a mad scramble for the ball. I spot it and reach for it, but a Rams lineman beats me to it by half a second.

The ref blows his whistle. "Green ball," he shouts.

We line up on defense and the Rams run out the clock. Twenty-eight to twenty-one. Our second loss in a row.

I look over to the bleachers for Ruby, but she and her friend are already gone.

Today the offense played well, but the defense didn't. This loss is on us.

CHAPTER 23

At lunch on Wednesday, Sam, Quincy, Noah, Dante, and Tony join our table to argue about offense versus defense.

"You wanted some points and we got you some points," Gig says. "We scored twenty-one, but that wasn't enough because the defense couldn't stop the Rams."

"We almost got the ball back for you in the final minute," I say. "Then we would have had a chance."

"Almost isn't good enough." Dante pours salsa on his nachos.

"The defense against the run was pretty good," Quincy says, "but they killed us with those short passes."

"Those short passes turned into long gains." Gig finishes off a bag of potato chips.

"Listen." Isaac holds up his hand. "We can't keep arguing. We're in this together. We need to act like a team."

"He's right," Diego says.

"We've got the Eagles next week." I crush my milk carton. "Everybody on that team goes to Eagle Bluff."

"Chickadee Bluff," Gig says. "We need to beat those chickadees."

"They're undefeated," Sam reminds him.

"I don't care." Gig stands up. "We're going to give them their first loss."

"And get our first victory," Tony adds.

"Longview." Gig points at me.

"Red Storm," I say back.

"Longview."

"Red Storm."

In American Studies, Mr. Lisicky points to the names of different American cities where Congress met, cities that can be considered early capitals of the United States.

Philadelphia, Pennsylvania

Baltimore, Maryland

Lancaster, Pennsylvania

York, Pennsylvania

Annapolis, Maryland

Trenton, New Jersey

New York, New York

"Not until 1800 did Congress meet in the newly established capital city of Washington, D.C. The city was named after President George Washington, who kept this disparate group of farmers, sailors, teamsters, shopkeepers, and booksellers together," he says. "Remember that the founding of this country isn't only about battles and dates. It's the story of people like Crispus Attucks, John Becker, and Henry and William Knox, some of whom were not much older than you are now."

Mr. Lisicky moves his arms as he gets into it. He's right. History is about people and their stories. That seems obvious, but I've never had a teacher make it so clear.

"The struggles of the American patriots were enormous and their chances of succeeding were low, but they risked their lives for liberty, for freedom," he says. "They persevered, and you are the beneficiaries of what they created. What are you doing with that precious freedom?"

I sit back and think about what I'm doing: going to school,

playing football, having fun with my friends. What do they call it in the Declaration of Independence? "Life, liberty, and the pursuit of happiness."

I'm pursuing happiness.

In FACS, I sit next to Ruby as our group reviews our checklist to see how many points Mrs. Randall gave us on our cheese bread lab.

"We lost a point on kitchen equipment cleanliness." Bossy Boots frowns. "Who's responsible for that?"

Caleb, the boy who likes to draw, raises his hand.

"What happened?" Bossy Boots leans toward him.

"Mrs. Randall said the knife wasn't clean enough." He draws a monster that resembles Bossy Boots in his notebook.

"Did you redo it?"

"Yeah, but she still took a point off."

Ruby smiles at me. We both know that arguing over one point is silly. "We still got thirty-two out of thirty-three," she says. "That's an A."

"We want all of them." Bossy Boots taps the paper.

"What we really wanted to do was eat cheese bread." I slide my chair toward Ruby.

"Yeah, and that was good," Caleb adds.

"Boys," Bossy Boots sneers. "All they're interested in is food."

"That's not all," Caleb says, and Ruby and I start laughing.

"What?" Caleb looks confused.

Bossy Boots frowns and goes back to her checklist.

"Are you still coming to the play on Friday night?" Ruby asks me.

"Yeah, I'll try."

Before practice, I try to persuade Isaac to come to the play with me, but he's doing something at his grandma's.

"What about you, Gig? Do you want to come to a play?"

"Come out to play what?" He boots a high punt to Sam.

"A play at school, a performance Friday night."

"Are you serious?"

"Yeah, I thought it might be interesting."

"Come on." He picks up another ball. "Who's in it that you want to see?"

"No one. I thought it might be fun."

"Yeah, right." He boots another high floater. "Who's in it?"

"Ruby Mallon. She's in my FACS lab.

"Ruby, Ruby, Ruby," Gig says in a high-pitched voice.

"Will you come?"

"No way. I'm going to the high school football game with Diego and his brother."

"Oh." That sounds a lot more fun than a play. I wonder if there's a way I can get out of it, but I told Ruby I'd come, and she held up her part of the deal by showing up at the game yesterday.

"Ruby, Ruby, Ruby," Gig calls.

He's perfected the art of being irritating.

I sit in the back of the auditorium on Friday night, and look around. I don't see anybody I know. It seems as if it's mostly family and friends of the performers. It's a different crowd from a football game. Not that many kids who are into sports are in plays, and not many kids who are in plays are into sports.

Mom asked me in the car who I knew in the play, and when I said Ruby Mallon, she said, "Oh, is that someone special we should know about?" That was embarrassing in front of Ted, Heather, and Haley. Still, I'd much rather be here than going to some dumb Disney movie with all of them. Honestly I'd rather be at the high school football game with Diego and Gig, but I don't think Mom would have allowed me to go to that. Not on a Heather and Haley weekend.

It's weird being here by myself, so I read through the program to have something to do. I skim through the cast members until I come to the name I'm here for: Ruby Mallon.

The lights go down and I lean back in my seat. When the play starts, I recognize a couple of sixth-grade guys who are wearing fake mustaches and are dressed in suits. I wouldn't volunteer to do that in a million years.

Then she appears. Ruby is wearing a red-and-white-checked dress and brown boots. Her hair is pulled back and tucked under an old-fashioned hat. She stands straight and tall. Some girls who are tall try to scrunch down a bit, but she's not like that.

"Good morning, sir, my name is Gwendolyn. Would you like to buy some eggs?" she says. I want to stand up and buy a dozen right there. I want to clap or yell the way you would at a football game. But instead I quietly watch her glide around the stage.

Meeting Ruby Mallon is the best thing about middle school so far.

CHAPTER 24

At the next meeting of READ Club, the tables are full and everybody is eating a bag lunch. We all did our homework because there are a lot more boys here, including Diego, Isaac, and Gig. I finally persuaded Gig to come by telling him he'd get out of advisory and there would be candy.

Some new girls have come, too, including Ruby, who was so happy I came to her play that she promised to come to another football game. She's sitting at a table with Kelsey and Sydney on the other side of the room since Gig automatically chose to sit as far away from Sydney as possible.

"This is much better." Mr. Amodt walks among the tables. "We're at about half and half now, which reflects the gender balance in the school."

Gig waves his hand.

"Yes," Mr. Amodt says.

"Jackson told me there would be candy here. I don't see any candy."

Sydney's shaking her head and Ruby's laughing.

"Trust me," Mr. Amodt says. "We've got lots of candy, but before we get to that, we've got a few things to do."

"We could have candy while we do them," Gig whispers.

"I'd like all of you who were here for the first meeting of READ Club and checked out books to tell the people at your table which books you liked best and why," Mr. Amodt says.

Since I'm the only one at my table who was at the last meeting, I hold up my copy of *The Boy Who Saved Baseball*. "I really liked this book. There's a cool character named Cruz de la Cruz and a baseball game where the stakes are huge. I didn't know what was going to happen and didn't want it to end."

"Is Cruz Mexican?" Diego asks.

"Yeah, and there's some Spanish in the book."

"Don't tell us more about it," Diego says. "I want to read it."

"Me, too," Isaac adds.

"I'll read it first." Gig takes it out of my hands. "I need a new book for reading lab."

"What about *The Desperado Who Stole Baseball*?" Isaac holds up the other book.

"That's the prequel to it, the one that came before."

"We know what a prequel is," Gig says. "Like in the movies."

Mr. Amodt comes over to our table and listens.

"It's about the outlaw Billy the Kid, and it's got a big surprise, too. I liked it so much I can't decide which is my favorite."

"Don't say any more." Diego holds up his hand. "I want to read it."

"I'll read it after you," Isaac says.

"That author has other books about baseball," Mr Amodt says. "When you find an author you connect with, it's like striking gold. You can read everything he or she has written."

"Do you really have lots of candy?" Gig asks.

"Tons of it," Mr. Amodt says. "I received a generous donation."

When it's time to look for new books, Gig and I automatically go to the sports table where Sam and Quincy are. I pick out a football book that has a great picture of a player breaking a tackle. Everybody says you can't judge a book by its cover, but I do it all the time.

Gig examines a nonfiction book about four-wheelers and dirt bikes. "My dad and I used to do this together."

"I saw the new picture of the two of you on the Wall of Heroes. It's cool."

"I like the regular picture of my dad better than the one in uniform. I know it's weird, but somehow that makes me feel like he won't get hurt."

"That's not weird."

"He called last night on Skype when Mom and Sydney were at the mall. I finally got to tell him about football and middle school without the two of them interrupting. He's doing okay and is counting the days until he's back here."

"Good."

Sam wants to see the pictures in Gig's book, so I pick up some other ones. At the next table, Ruby's comparing covers. "What are you looking for?"

"I like historical fiction," she says. "I like learning what it was like to live in different times."

"Like in the play."

"Yeah." She turns over a book called A *Single Shard* and adds it to her pile.

"I just read a book set in another time."

"Really?"

I start telling her about *The Desperado Who Stole Baseball*, and she listens while she looks at me with her big eyes that never seem to blink.

"Be brave," Mr. Amodt announces. "Step out of your comfort zone. If you always read fantasy, try some realistic fiction. If you always read mysteries, try some nonfiction." He sees me at the historical fiction table and nods. He doesn't realize I'm only here because of Ruby.

I pick up a copy of a book called *Brooklyn Bridge* and read the description on the back, which sounds interesting. "I'll try this." I add it to my other book.

"I'll read it after you and we can discuss it." Ruby walks over toward the sports table. "And I'll pick one from here." She chooses a book called *The Girl Who Threw Butterflies*.

"I'll read it after you." I hold out my hand. "Deal?"

"Deal," she says. We shake in her dramatic fashion, and I like how her hand feels against mine.

Before the game against the Eagles, Coach Martineau is pacing back and forth in front of us. "We need to work together today, offense, defense, special teams. The Eagles are good. Don't kid yourselves. But we can be good, too. We need everybody involved. When the offense is on the field, we want the defense supporting them. When the defense is on, we want the offense cheering for them."

I finger the pad on my splint. I'm ready for the kickoff.

"You all go to the same school, Longview Middle School," Coach says. "You're not fifth graders from different elementary schools anymore. You're sixth graders from one school—Longview."

Coach is right. So much has happened in the time we've been in middle school that elementary school seems like years ago.

"Let's go out there and have fun," Coach says. "Let's go out there and get a win."

"Yeah!" we all shout.

"Hands in." Coach sticks his out and we all extend an arm. I pull my wrapped hand back and put the other one in.

"One, two, three," Coach counts.

"LONGVIEW!"

We start out on offense, and on the first play from scrimmage, Isaac fakes the end around and keeps it himself for a gain of nineteen.

"Way to run," Diego hollers.

"Nice gain," I shout.

Gig offers Isaac a hand up and they jog back to the huddle together. Over on the bleachers, Mom, Ted, and Quinn sit together. Across the way, Dad's standing next to Isaac's dad, and G-Man's talking to a short man in a baseball hat that I recognize.

"Diego." I point. "Your dad's here."

Diego smiles. "He better not tell my mom about your hand."

I turn to the bleachers again and *she* is here. Ruby is climbing the stairs with Sydney and Kelsey. She's come to two games in a row.

On first and ten, Isaac drops back to pass and floats one to Gig. An Eagles linebacker sniffs it out and stops him after a gain of two.

"Way to go, Gundy," one of the Eagles coaches shouts.

It's Cole Gunderson, who played baseball with us on the Panthers.

On the next play, Isaac pitches to Gig, who tries to get outside. Two Eagles cut him off, so he stops and turns back the other way. Isaac throws a block on Cole, and Gig dashes all the way to the other sideline for a gain of three.

"That was a long way to run for a little yardage," Diego says.

"Yeah, but it's better than a loss." I clap. "Way to go, Gig."

On the next play, Isaac drops back to pass, but nobody is open. He steps up in the pocket and looks for Dante, but he's covered, too. Isaac pulls the ball down and takes off running. He sidesteps Steve Stein, who also played baseball with us, and picks up twenty yards.

We're all jumping up and down on the sideline while Cole and Steve argue with each other about who's responsible for containing the quarterback.

"Go, Red Storm." It's funny to see former teammates trying to stop us.

On the next play, Isaac hands off to Gig, who breaks off tackle and bounces outside. He fakes Cole out so badly that Cole ends up grabbing air as he falls over backward. Gig tears downfield and beats Steve to the end zone.

The referee blows his whistle and holds up his hands. Touchdown.

We all yell and cheer, but the referee pulls out a penalty flag from his pocket and tosses it high in the air.

How can there be a penalty? He already signaled touchdown.

"What happened? What happened?" Coach Martineau steps out onto the field.

"Unsportsmanlike conduct at the end of the play on number forty-three. Taunting. Fifteen-yard penalty to be assessed on the kickoff." He raises both arms. "Touchdown."

Taunting? What did Gig say?

"Milroy, get over here." Coach sends in a sub for the extra point.

"I didn't say anything," Gig says as he jogs off the field.

"You must have said something." Coach pulls Gig's jersey. "You got a taunting penalty."

"I didn't say any words," Gig says.

"What did you do then?"

"I just went *tweet, tweet, tweet*."

Coach looks like he's halfway between exploding and cracking up. "Keep your mouth shut next time you score." He slaps Gig's shoulder pads.

I can't help smiling. Who but Gig would think to make chickadee noises for the Eagles?

On defense, Diego stops the first play for no gain all by himself.

"You're the man, Padre," Gig shouts.

"I told you you'd be good." I pull Diego up and he's smiling.

On second and ten, they try a quick pitch, but I'm ready

for it and string it out. When the running back tries to cut in, Nick Speros tackles him for a loss.

"Good work," I say.

"You, too." Nick gives me a fist bump.

On the next play, Coach Tanglen signals for the stunt Diego and I practiced.

"Meet you at the quarterback," I say as we line up.

"Down, set, hut." The quarterback drops back to pass.

Diego bulls outside and creates an opening for me. I bounce off my guy and squeeze through. I rush the quarterback who's got his arm back. He sees me coming and tucks the ball in and rolls out. Diego's beaten both his guys to the outside. The quarterback turns around and I slam my shoulder into his chest and tackle him into Diego's open arms, and all three of us fall to the ground.

"Way to go, Diego," G-Man shouts. "Way to go, Jackson."

Diego offers me a hand and pulls me up. On the sideline, my dad, Isaac's dad, and Diego's dad are clapping. I turn to the bleachers and see Mom, Ted, and Quinn standing and cheering. And Kelsey, Sydney, and Ruby are on their feet, too.

I adjust the pad on my hand as I line up for the next play. I love this game.

CHAPTER 25

After our thirty-one to fourteen win over the Eagles, we celebrate on the field.

"Longview Red Storm, Longview Red Storm," Gig chants and we all join in. "Longview Red Storm, Longview Red Storm."

Coach Martineau raises his arm. "Line up to shake hands."

"Good game, man." Cole Gunderson slaps my shoulder pads.

"You, too."

"We'll beat you next time," Steve Stein says. "We'll kill you in basketball."

"No way. Not as long as we've got Isaac."

After we finish the line, we gather around the coaches.

"Great game," Coach Martineau says. "You played like a team."

"We're going to play like that the rest of the season," Coach Tanglen joins in.

I believe him as I look around at my teammates. It took us a while to quit arguing between offense and defense, but now that we're together and we see what we can do, we're going to be good.

Isaac and Gig congratulate Diego and me. "Great game by the defense."

"The offense was good, too," I say.

"The team was great," Diego says.

I turn to the bleachers where Ruby is talking with Sydney and Kelsey. I'm so glad she was here to see the win.

"One other announcement." Coach Martineau turns to Gig. "Milroy, for that taunting penalty, you have four laps around the field tomorrow, and you're going to make bird-calls the entire way."

We all laugh and Gig grins.

"Enjoy the win," Coach Tanglen says. "Remember this feeling."

I watch Ruby across the way hanging out with Sydney and Kelsey. She's looking my way, but I can't do anything with Gig, Isaac, and Diego standing here.

Mom comes up with Ted and I cross my arms. I don't

want her giving me a hug or doing something embarrassing in front of everybody.

"I was worried about your hand every time you made a tackle," she says. "How is it?"

"Fine." I hold it up.

"That's nerve-wracking to watch, but I'm glad you won."

Ted grins broadly. "Good game."

"Thanks."

We stand around making small talk before Mom gets in a couple more reminders about protecting my hand and getting to bed early on a school night.

"Yeah."

She and Ted walk arm in arm to his car. No Heather or Haley. No Quinn or me. Just the two of them.

My teammates say good-bye and drift off. Isaac goes with his dad and Diego with his. Gig's the only one of us who didn't have a dad here. That's got to be tough. That must be why he's been having such a hard time lately. He'd want his dad to see his touchdown. Maybe not the tweet-tweet-tweet penalty, though.

Quinn races over and jumps up on me. "You're a star."

"What about me?" Gig asks.

"You're always a star."

"Smart kid." Gig hands Quinn his helmet. "Good somebody in the family got some brains."

G-Man rushes up. "Now that was a football game."

"You and Diego worked well together," Dad says.

"Timed that stunt perfectly," G-Man adds. "Diego's dad had a lot of questions, but he enjoyed his first football game."

I look over at Ruby, who's walking away from the field with Sydney and Kelsey.

"What happened on that taunting penalty?" G-Man asks.

Gig starts telling the story and I see my chance.

"I'll be right back." I hand my helmet to Dad and run over to Ruby who's hung back from Sydney and Kelsey.

"Congratulations," she says.

"Thanks." I rub the sweat from my forehead.

"I don't know much about football, but you played really well."

"Thanks." I look at her clear, smooth skin and her bright eyes and try to figure out what I should say.

"Doesn't it hurt when you crash into the guy with the ball?"

"Nah." I shake my head. "That feels great."

"Looks like it hurts."

"Nah, that's why we wear all this padding." The sun dips down into a cloud that hugs the horizon.

"I could never do that in a million years," Ruby says.

"Well, I could never memorize lines and stand up on a stage with everybody watching."

We talk about football and school, and I'm amazed how the words flow.

Kelsey's mom honks the horn and Kelsey hollers for Ruby.

"I got to go," she says.

"Me, too. Thanks, Ruby, for coming."

"My pleasure." She steps forward and bows like an actress. She waves at me as she runs and I wave to her.

As I walk back, I soak up the good feelings. I don't care if Gig gives me a hard time about Ruby. He's just jealous because no girl came to watch him. Nobody but Sydney and Kelsey, and he sure wouldn't count them.

I'm excited about going to school tomorrow and hearing people talk about the game. I'm excited to discuss different plays with my teammates. I'm excited to see Ruby and talk some more with her.

I never thought I'd get to this point, but I'm excited to be in middle school. I'm excited about Longview.

Acknowledgments

*E*very book involves research, and for this one, I broke my thumb. Thanks to Doctor Cherrie Heinrich and Occupational Therapist Nhu Wong for helping me heal.

Thanks to the teachers and students at Valley Middle School for answering questions and allowing me access. Particular thanks to counselors Linda Prince and John Brickner for their guidance.

Thanks to Liz Szabla, Jean Feiwel, Elizabeth Fithian, Rich Deas, Lizzy Mason, Dave Barrett, Anne Heausler, and everybody at Feiwel and Friends. What a team!

Thanks to my All-Star agent, Andrea Cascardi, and the writers of KTM, who put points on the board.

Thanks to everyone at Echo Park Elementary School, especially Sally Soliday, Paula Kranz, and Judy Zarn, and to teachers Dan Dudley and Kim Coleman and their students for their insights, questions, and enthusiasm.

Thanks to Principal Kim Hill and everyone at Flynn Elementary School, particularly Cheryl Lawrence and Matt Wigdahl and their fifth-grade students for their excellent suggestions.